Forsaking All Others
Addan & Nicole

Darrell and Nakesha White

Forsaking All Others
Copyright © 2024 Darrell and Nakesha White

Books may be purchased in quantity and/or special sales by contacting the publishers, Darrell and Nakesha White, by email at darrelldrwhite@gmail.com.

First Edition

Published in the United States of America by Darell and Nakesha White

Table of Contents

Chapter 1

Addan stared down into Nicole's eyes. This was the best day of his life. After all he had gone through as a man, he could finally say he'd chosen well. Things hadn't worked out with his last two marriages, but after a process of healing, he emerged stronger and more aware than he was with his ex-wives.

A pang of hurt flashed through him at the thought of Damiyah, his second ex-wife, but he knew she would be okay. They had gone through a painful, yet amicable divorce. The painful part was because neither of them wanted their marriage to end, but the amicable part was because they both knew their decision was the best one for themselves and their two children. Addan shot a glance at his son and daughter sitting in the front row, then nodded at Briana, Nicole's daughter.

Briana gave him an uneasy smile and fidgeted in her seat, while Addan's sons, Addan Jr. and Michael, beamed at him from his seats. Addan Jr. was born during his first marriage to his ex-wife, Niya, and Michael and Makiyah were born during his second marriage to Damiyah. Makiyah was on her cell phone but seemed to sense her father's gaze. She looked up and gave him a guilty smile before putting her phone away. Addan nodded, then questioned his decision not to invite Damiyah to him and Nicole's nuptials, but he reasoned she probably would have declined anyway. Though Damiyah had dated a few men since their divorce, Addan had to admit that inviting her to their wedding would have been a bit much. They got along so well it was like they were brother and sister, but every relationship had its boundaries.

"The rings, please?"

Addan licked his lips and straightened his stance as he refocused on Nicole.

She was staring up at him wearing much of the same nervous smile as her daughter had. Addan made a mental note to tease her about it later. Nobody could tell Nicole she didn't spit that girl out. It was almost like they were twins, though Briana was only sixteen and her mother was in her thirties.

Addan and Nicole exchanged rings and recited their vows. His heart beat wildly in his chest as he awaited the next part.

Pastor Solomon spoke in a solemn tone. "By the grace and mercy of our Lord Jesus Christ, I now pronounce you husband and wife. Addan, you may kiss your bride."

Addan took a deep breath, then lifted Nicole's veil.

Gone was her nervous smile and now it was replaced with the radiant confidence he had grown to admire. Her perfectly straight white teeth gleamed in his direction as he lowered his head to kiss her.

When their lips touched, Addan felt the same spark of electricity he felt the first time they shared a kiss, only this time it was intensified. It was as if God himself had orchestrated their relationship to culminate in this day, and Addan knew in his heart it would only get better from here.

The attendees let out a hearty applause as Addan and Nicole finished their kiss, then they turned to face everyone as the organist played a tune.

Addan's buddy Leonard dropped the broom before them, and Nicole lifted her dress before she and Addan counted together. "One... two... three!"

They jumped in unison amidst another round of applause, then made their way down the aisle to their limo.

The wedding planner had done a magnificent job with the reception hall decor. Addan's smile grew wider as he recalled the conversation he had with the woman. Since he had been married before, he didn't want to go all out for this wedding. He wanted things to be presentable but not kill his budget. After all, it was more about the marriage than the wedding. Pastor Solomon had drilled this into him and Nicole's heads as they attended premarital counseling before their big day. Addan couldn't have agreed more. Nicole didn't seem to mind not throwing a lavish affair either, though she had never been married.

"I'm a minimalist, baby," she said when Addan expressed his concern. "Whatever the budget, I'm sure Kamisha can make it work. She's the best."

His wife was right, because Addan was blown away at how Kamisha had pulled off such extravagant-looking centerpieces, wedding favors, and other items on a wedding that cost less than three thousand dollars, outside his tux and Nicole's dress.

Nicole's dress was the only thing she wanted to splurge on. She had a vision in her mind since she was a girl of how she wanted it to look, so Addan agreed that his wife should have what she wanted, especially since she didn't kill his pockets with the wedding itself.

After all expenses were paid, Addan and Nicole still had a sizable saving's account, and that was what mattered the most to him.

Addan and Nicole sat in the center of the head table of the reception hall with their parents, bridesmaids, and groomsmen on either side of them.

Before he knew it, the party was underway. The dining tables were placed on the edges of the floor to make room for people to dance in the middle.

At first, people just mingled while sipping on drinks and appetizers, then when the DJ played more upbeat music, one of Nicole's family members started dancing. It didn't take long for everyone to join in.

Everyone except Addan's daughter, Makiyah. Instead of joining the festivities with her brothers, Makiyah was sitting in her seat staring at Nicole with a look that would split her in half if she had the power.

Addan's forehead creased at the sight of that. What was Makiyah's deal? As far as he knew, she and Nicole hadn't had any disagreements lately.

He made a mental note to talk about it, then relaxed, brushing it off.

It was probably nothing.

Chapter 2

Nicole could not believe how blessed she was.

After a rocky past with relationships, including the arduous trial she endured with Briana's father, Breon, Nicole was ready to swear off love and relationships completely. She hadn't entertained a man for years, then the loneliness set in. Why should she have been forced to spend the rest of her life alone because of a few bad seeds?

After careful thought, Nicole joined a Christian dating app. She figured it would be just for fun at first, a chance to meet a few men and see if the dating pool was truly full of pee as social media trends seemed to insist.

After a few conversations with men of different ages and backgrounds, Nicole was ready to delete the app and continue her single carefree life.

Then she met Addan, and he turned her world upside down.

Addan showed Nicole a side of men she had never experienced. For starters, he respected her. When she presented boundaries, he stayed within them. When they went on dates, he opened doors, pushed in chairs, and took care of every outing, barely letting her leave the tips.

Then came the fact that he was a man of his word. Nicole had been with a few men who told her one thing but did the opposite, but not so for Addan. Everything he told her about himself was proven to be true through his actions. If he said he would do something, he did it. If they had to be somewhere on time, they made it. If something was important to Nicole, he made it a priority for himself too.

Addan was almost the perfect man. Nicole knew no man was truly perfect, but she thanked God that hers was close enough.

She still had a few days left in her vacation from work, so she focused on rearranging things in Addan's house and binge-watching housewife shows.

Nicole had moved into Addan's home for practical reasons. She had a two bedroom apartment while he had a four bedroom home that he had previously shared with his ex-wife Damiyah and their two children, Michael and Makiyah.

At first, Nicole was reluctant to move into a house that another woman had lived in, but she was later convinced it made sense. Why would she have Addan move out of his house if it held enough space for her and her daughter to live there? Especially since Addan went out of his way to give Briana Addan Jr.'s room that he used on weekends, while converting an office space into a bedroom for his oldest son.

"I need to start seeing this as our house, not just his," she mused, then turned the TV up. Just as she was getting to the good part in the episode, a key turned in the lock on the front door.

Nicole's eyes shot to the wall clock above the flatscreen TV. Addan wasn't off work yet, and the kids should still be in school...

Before she could form the assumption that Addan had left work early to spend some time together, Nicole was met with the shock of her life.

She had only seen her in pictures and spoken to her briefly on the phone, but Damiyah's smug smile could not be mistaken.

Nicole sprang up from the couch after putting the TV on mute.

"What are you doing here?"

Damiyah's smirk deepened as she continued to invade the home. "What do you mean, what am I doing here? It's my house."

Nicole's mind was scrambling. "No, this is not your house, Damiyah. Did Addan arrange for you to come pick up the kids or something? I'm not understanding why you're here."

Damiyah was busy walking around and looking at everything as if inspecting it. "I'm just making sure my home is being taken care of."

Nicole's territorial instincts kicked in. "Listen, honey. I don't want any issues with you. The kids aren't due home for at least another hour, so if that's what you came for, I'm going to ask that you come back later, and I'm going to need the key you used to walk in the door."

Nicole wondered why Damiyah had a key in the first place. Yes, she had lived there with Addan and the kids when they were married, but their divorce had long been finalized. Why hadn't Addan taken back the key?

Chills ran down her spine at the possible reasons, but Nicole didn't allow her mind to go there. Addan had never given her reason to suspect he was cheating, and she wasn't going to project her past relationships onto him.

Damiyah fixed her with a stank expression. "Give back the key? Why would I do that?"

Nicole stood her ground. "Because this is my home that I share with my husband. There is no need for you to have a key. You can knock when you come to pick up the kids just like any other visitor."

The women stared each other down, neither relenting on their position.

After a few moments, Nicole grabbed her cell phone and called Addan on speaker. Her first thought was to call the police, but she didn't want to go that route unless she had to.

"Hello?" he answered on the second ring.

"Addan," Nicole said, forcing a neutral tone as Damiyah continued to stare her down. "Damiyah is here. I'm not sure if you guys arranged for her to pick up the kids, but she used a key to walk in, and she's saying she's not leaving." Nicole hoped her husband was picking up everything she was putting down because they would certainly have a conversation about the key later.

"What?" Addan's shock-filled tone sounded on the line. "What do you mean she walked in using a key? Can I speak with her?"

"You're on speaker," Nicole said in as calm of a tone as she could muster.

"Damiyah?" Addan said.

Damiyah gave Nicole another mischievous grin. "Yes?"

"What's going on? You're not supposed to take the kids until tonight."

"Oh, am I?" she said in a fake-sweet tone. "I must have been mistaken. Let me come back later then."

"Okay," Addan said, sounding confused at her gesture.

Damiyah approached the door.

"Leave the key," Nicole said, but Damiyah ignored her and walked out, leaving the door wide open.

Nicole seethed as she stalked over and watched Damiyah sashay to her car, get inside, and pull off. She didn't know what the hell that woman's issue was, but Nicole was not about to deal with it. Nicole returned her attention to her husband, who was still on speakerphone. "We need to talk when you get home."

Chapter 3

Addan took several deep breaths as he approached his front door. He had a long day at work outside of the drama with Nicole and Damiyah.

For the life of him, he couldn't understand why his ex-wife had done such a thing. Had he said something to upset her? Why would Damiyah barge into their house, knowing full well that they had an agreement about boundaries as soon as things became serious between him and Nicole?

He had half a mind to turn around and go back to his car but knew he couldn't. He could only hope that Nicole would take it easy on him and let him explain.

He unlocked the door and entered their home, seeing Nicole sitting on the couch with a cold expression on her face, watching TV.

From the sounds in the atmosphere, the kids were upstairs in their rooms which meant it was undoubtedly discussion time. He let out a short breath. "How was your day?"

Nicole's stony expression remained fixated on the TV. Addan stepped out of his dress shoes, then put them in the shoe rack that Nicole had neatly set up earlier that week. He carried his briefcase to his office down the hall, storing it on his desk and locking the door before returning to the living room to engage with his stewing wife.

He sat next to her on the couch and grabbed one of her feet, starting a massage.

Nicole loved massages. She stiffened at his touch, then as he continued, he felt her relax. She turned to face him. "Why did she have a key, Addan?"

There it was. The question he knew was coming. He hoped she bought his explanation because it was the truth.

"Babe, we both had keys to each other's homes after the divorce because it was convenient. Although we were no longer together, it was easier to manage things. Plus, we would sometimes have family nights over at her apartment or this house. That's all it was. We established a boundary once you and I got serious, though. Damiyah has not used her key since you and I became official, and I forgot I even had one to her apartment."

Nicole sat in silence for a few moments, seemingly taking in his words. "I don't like the idea of her still having access to our home. She made a few comments when she was here that rubbed me the wrong way."

Addan halted his massage. "What kinds of comments?"

He listened as his wife explained how Damiyah waltzed around like she owned the place and disrespected Nicole by ignoring her request for the key when she left.

"Wow," he said, not believing his ears. "I never would have expected something like this from her. Everything was cool between us before. I don't know what could have..." He trailed off.

"I do," Nicole said softly, then peered into his eyes. "She's obviously not happy we're married, Addan."

Those words were like a punch in the gut. Was Nicole right? If she was, Addan didn't know how he would proceed. Things went smoothly when everyone was on board with their arrangement. Addan had been proud to say he never had to deal with baby momma drama like other guys. Now it seemed things would all be left in shambles unless he and Damiyah had a serious conversation.

"How about this?" Addan said, a new sense of resolve flowing through him. "I'll call a locksmith in the morning and get the locks changed. It will be a pain in the butt, but we need to do it anyway. I'll have a discussion with Damiyah to see what she's thinking. How do you like that?"

Nicole looked worried. "Addan, that sounds great. I just... I really don't want to deal with any ex-related drama. I've been through too much in my life to deal with this now."

Addan understood completely, and he fully agreed. "Don't worry, babe. I'm sure we can smooth things over and be back to normal in no time."

Addan and Nicole were back to normal by the end of the night. They slept peacefully, and Addan almost forgot Damiyah was supposed to pick up the kids until she texted him. She said she had some things to take care of so she would pick them up the next day after school. Addan agreed and secretly planned to get off work early so they could have a conversation. He didn't want drama with Damiyah if he could help it, and he certainly didn't want issues with his new wife either. Hopefully they could handle this like adults.

The next morning, Addan thought of an even better idea: some of the furniture he previously shared with Damiyah was still in the house. There were a few pieces Nicole mentioned wanting recently, so he surprised her by taking the day off work and going furniture shopping with his wife while also getting the locks changed.

Nicole was like a kid in a candy store picking out pieces she wanted for their living room and dining room. The more time they spent carefully choosing their new furniture, the more Addan felt he had made the right decision.

The company had same-day delivery, and as luck would have it, the locksmith he contacted was able to come out that same day too, so Addan and Nicole killed two birds with one stone.

Damiyah showed up promptly on time after school to pick up the kids while Nicole was in the shower washing away the day's activities.

Addan opened his mouth to mention that he wanted to speak with her, but she seemed to be in a rush. "Okay, kids tell your father you'll see him later!"

"Bye, Daddy!" Mikayah and Michael said in unison, and Damiyah whisked them away. Addan wondered what the hurry was all about, but he didn't have time to think much of it because when he turned back around after locking the door, Nicole was standing in the middle of the living room wearing a fluffy pink bathrobe and a seductive smile.

"How about we christen our new couch?" she asked, and then let the robe fall to the floor.

***

Addan's weekend turned out better than expected. Their first official weekend as husband and wife, and he and Nicole had been together in almost every room in the house. He almost wanted to take a week off work to recuperate.

Chuckling at the thought, he remembered that Damiyah was due to drop the kids off by dinner time tonight. It was Sunday.

He turned to his wife with a lazy smile. "Do you think we should order in tonight?"

She gave him a mischievous look of her own. "Again?" Then she shrugged. "I don't see why not."

Addan shot a quick text to Damiyah, asking her to ask the kids what they wanted for dinner, then took a shower with his wife.

When they emerged an hour later, skin wrinkled but both feeling refreshed, Addan checked his phone to see that Damiyah still hadn't written back.

Was her phone off? Addan wrinkled his nose and called her. It rang eight times before going to voicemail.

"What's wrong?" Nicole said, noticing her husband's confusion.

"Damiyah isn't answering. I texted her before we got in the shower to find out what the kids wanted to order for dinner, and she didn't write back. I just tried to call her too, but she didn't respond."

Nicole stared at him. "Do you think she might be on her way?"

Addan shrugged but couldn't ignore the sinking feeling in his gut. "I don't know. I hope she's not playing more games." Now that the words escaped his lips, Nicole seemed worried about the same thing.

"I'm sure it will be fine," she said.

But two more hours passed and still no Damiyah.

Addan grew frantic. He called and texted a dozen more times, wondering what could have happened. Had they gotten into an accident? Was someone in the hospital? Where were Damiyah and the kids? Why wasn't she answering?

As Nicole was in the middle of calming Addan's worries, Damiyah finally sent a text.

Hey. Sorry so late. The kids and I had so much fun that they want to spend the night. I'll bring them to school in the morning.

Addan grew furious as he read the message because it meant Damiyah had ignored his calls and texts just as he thought she did.

Nicole stepped in again. "It is kind of late, Addan. Why not just let them spend the night this once? Maybe it will help smooth out whatever issue Damiyah had the other day."

Addan disagreed and wanted his kids home, even if he had to take the two hour drive to get them himself, but he forced himself to relax.

"I guess you're right," he said.

The next day, Addan went through his normal work day, then went to pick up the kids from school. He sat outside watching all the grade levels as they dismissed, but Mikayah nor Michael walked out the doors.

Figuring they must have been late, he waited ten more minutes.

When it seemed the last of the kids had come outside, but his son and daughter were nowhere to be found, the unsettled feeling Addan experienced earlier returned. He exited his vehicle and signed in to the school, requesting to speak with his children's teachers. They came around the same time and what they told him caused Addan's heart to drop to his knees.

"I'm sorry, Mr. Roberts. We thought Michael and Mikayah's last day was Friday. We threw them a going away party and everything. Are you saying you didn't know?"

Addan's mind filled with shock. "Going away party?" he repeated. "What do you mean, going away party? Where were they going?"

Michael's teacher stepped forward. "Their mother has been emailing us for weeks about it. We all planned the party together. I could have sworn you were CC'd." She whipped out her phone and then wrinkled her nose, then her eyes widened. "Yes, this is your email address right here!" She showed it to him.

Addan's mind swirled before rage filled his veins. It was his email address, all right, but it was from a decade ago, and Damiyah knew that.

"Can I speak with the principal?" he asked, attempting to regain some semblance of control over the situation.

Unfortunately, the only thing the principal could do was confirm what the teachers had already told him. "I'm truly sorry, Mr. Roberts. You and Ms. Nichols always seemed to be on the same page. We had no clue you didn't know she was moving them."

Addan didn't know how he made it out of that school without falling apart.

Damiyah had taken his children.

Addan's body became wracked with emotions he didn't recognize. There was no way she could do this, was there?

He called Damiyah's phone, and this time, she answered with a nonchalant tone. "Hello?"

"Damiyah, what the hell is going on?" Addan's voice raised several octaves as he spoke. "I just left the kids' school, and they told me you moved them. What are you doing? We never discussed this!"

Damiyah spoke her next words in a nice-nasty tone. "You mean you didn't see the emails? We've been planning this for weeks."

"Damiyah, you know damn well I didn't see those emails. You did this behind my back. I can't believe you! What school did you put them in?"

"I placed our children in one of the best schools in our area. Two blocks from my apartment."

"But you know there's no way I'll be able to pick them up from school on time. And then their after-school activities…"

Damiyah cut him off. "My children have been signed up for new after school activities. And you don't have to worry about picking them up. I have that taken care of."

Addan grew dizzy. "What are you saying, Damiyah?"

Her next words were a dagger to his heart. "I'm saying the kids are staying with me, and we can arrange for you to see them on the weekends."

Chapter 4

Nicole picked her daughter up from school like usual, but when they got home, Addan was there, pacing the living room floor. After taking one look at her husband, Nicole immediately picked up that something was wrong.

"What happened?" she asked, and when she saw the wounded look in his eyes, it pricked her heart. "Briana, baby, can you go upstairs while Addan and I talk?"

Briana didn't need to be told twice. Her soft footsteps ascended to her bedroom.

Nicole turned back to Addan. "What happened?"

Addan's fists were balled, and his breathing was labored. He stood stark still with a blank expression on his face.

"Addan, you're scaring me. What is it?" She took a step closer as Addan mumbled. "What did you say?"

"I said she took my kids, Nicole!"

His sharp tone startled her, but Nicole was at a loss for words as she took in what Addan had just told her. "What do you mean, she took the kids?"

Addan regained his composure and told her what happened when he went to pick up Michael and Mikayah from school.

Nicole clapped a hand over her mouth. "Oh my God..." Visions of her ex, Breon, filled Nicole's mind, but she focused on the matter at hand.

She felt horrible for her husband and wished there was something she could do. "Let me talk to her," she offered.

"Huh?"

"Let me talk to her, Addan. What's her number?"

Addan blinked back tears and handed Nicole his phone. Nicole found Damiyah's name in the contacts and then dialed the number on her own cell phone. Maybe the element of surprise would cause the woman to snap out of whatever drama she was getting sucked into.

"Hello?" Damiyah answered on the fourth ring.

"Hi, Damiyah. It's Nicole."

"Nicole who?" she said in a snarky tone, knowing full well who she was.

Nicole kept calm. "Addan's wife. He just told me what happened. Can we have a conversation, please?"

"What conversation?" Damiyah said, playing dumb.

Nicole let out a breath. "A conversation about why you moved the children without their father's knowledge. We don't want problems, Damiyah. We just want to—"

Damiyah cut her off. "If you don't want problems, you can stop calling my phone. Addan has my number. He knows how to get into contact with me."

"Damiyah, come on. You're not being fair in this situation, and you know it. Can we please talk to the children?"

"Addan can talk to the kids on Friday when I bring them out there. Don't call my phone again."

The line went dead.

Nicole felt more defeated than her husband and that was saying something because Addan seemed like he was on the verge of losing it.

"Listen, honey," she soothed, grabbing his hands, and trying to calm him. "How about we give her the week to cool off then try to talk to her on Friday?"

"Nicole, she moved the kids to a new school! She already set them up with after school programs and everything. This was not the arrangement we had, and she knows it! She's doing this out of spite."

Nicole knew that feeling all too well, and every word out of Addan's mouth was true, but she had to find a way to keep him calm because like it or not, the only thing the police would say if they called them was to take the situation to court. Nicole knew that from experience.

"I know it's hard, but we'll find a way to work this out, Addan. Let's talk to Damiyah on Friday and see where her head is at."

Addan seemed to accept those words, but he was on pins and needles the rest of the week. When Friday rolled around, Nicole and Addan were waiting at the door for Damiyah to bring the kids. She brought them on time, but as Addan and Nicole walked toward her car to begin a conversation, she drove off like she didn't see them.

Nicole was growing sick of that woman already, but she put on a nice face for Addan and the kids.

"How about we do a game night?" she asked, her eyes widening with forced excitement.

Addan nodded in agreement, and Michael clapped and jumped up and down at the idea, but Mikayah continued into the house acting like she didn't hear the suggestion. Addan Jr. arrived sometime later, and he was completely oblivious to the turmoil his father was facing.

Nicole's heart sank. It seemed that things were about to get rocky from here.

Chapter 5

Nicole tossed and turned the entire night after Michael and Mikayah came home. Addan snored peacefully beside her. It was like they had switched mindsets. He was calm now that the kids were home, and Nicole was the one in a frenzy because of how Mikayah was acting. Addan didn't seem to notice that something was wrong when his daughter declined the game night. Instead, she lounged on the couch scrolling her cell phone while Briana, Michael, Addan, Addan Jr., and Nicole played Monopoly.

She spoke to her brothers and father and was polite to Briana, but Mikayah didn't look in Nicole's direction the entire night. When Nicole offered to fix everyone's plates of pizza and soda, everyone shouted their orders, but Mikayah said nothing.

Nicole left her alone, figuring she must be adjusting to the new norm of living with her mom fulltime and seeing her father on the weekends.

In her heart, Nicole suspected that the transition wasn't the only thing on Mikayah's mind—it was something much deeper, but she wasn't the girl's mother, so she felt it wasn't her place to complain. She reasoned she would give it a few weeks and hopefully things would clear up between them.

After Nicole had brought everyone except Mikayah food and drinks, she turned to ask her one last time if she wanted something, but Mikayah promptly stood from the couch and disappeared into the kitchen, returning with a plate of pizza and a cup of soda that she fixed herself.

Nicole looked at Addan, but he was engrossed in his conversation with Michael, Addan Jr., and Briana. Nicole was thankful that Mikayah at least seemed to get along with her daughter, so she didn't mention it.

But now that she was trying to settle down for the night, her mind became filled with painful memories of her ex, Breon and all she had endured as a result of him.

Nicole hoped the Damiyah situation wouldn't be a repeat of all she had to go through, but judging from how Damiyah was acting, a court date was likely in their near future.

Then it would begin all over again.

Nicole thought she was finished with court dates. She had been before so many judges, the courts knew her by name. Anxiety flooded her heart as her throat constricted with swelling emotion.

"Please, Lord, no. Please cause Damiyah to snap out of it and handle things like an adult rather than play games. Lord, spare us from having to go through the court system."

Though her prayer was sincere, Nicole had the sinking suspicion that Damiyah was ready for war.

Chapter 6

Addan hated that it had to come to this, but if Damiyah wanted a fight, he would give her one. She had no right to take their children out of the home and school system they had been in all their lives because she wanted to act like a bitter baby momma.

Maybe referring to her in that way was out of line, but Addan had it with Damiyah's antics as well as her refusal to talk to him. He couldn't understand where things went wrong. Before he married Nicole, everything moved smoothly, and they functioned as a unit. Even after he and Nicole became serious, Damiyah never let on that she had a problem.

Then as soon as they got married, all hell broke loose. It was as if she had smiled in their faces this whole time just to pounce directly after the wedding. Obviously, her plan was in motion long before Addan caught wind of it, especially with the calculated way she sent those emails to the principal and the kids' teachers while CC'ing his old email address. Didn't she understand the ones who were suffering the most from her actions were the kids? Michael and Mikayah were excelling where they were at. Addan had prided himself over the fact that he and Damiyah didn't have to go to the courts to arrange a custody agreement when they got divorced. Now he wished they would have.

"Mr. Roberts, how are you?" Jessica Benson, Addan's lawyer, greeted him.

They shook hands. "Hopefully better once this situation gets resolved."

Addan watched as Nicole and Jessica shook hands next.

Nicole appeared more worried than he was about how things would work out. When Addan mentioned that he was hiring a lawyer, Nicole's expression changed as if she had become visibly sick, and Addan wondered what that was about. Did his wife think he was making the wrong decision by bringing Damiyah to court? Addan wanted to ask but didn't want to rock the boat. Plus, these were his kids. They had been under his care their entire life. He had always been the more hands on parent, attending every PTO meeting, every school event, and the list went on. How dare Damiyah pull a stunt like this?

"Mr. Roberts?" Jessica said, jolting him back to attention.

"Huh? I'm sorry, Jessica. What were you saying?"

She smiled as if understanding his distractedness. "I was saying I'm confident we can turn this situation around for you. It's good that you came to me quickly, and from everything you shared on the phone, I think we have a solid case."

"Don't they always side with the mother, though?" Nicole blurted, then looked down as if she were ashamed when Addan glared at her.

Jessica paused before speaking again. "In many cases, yes, the courts do side with the mother, but if we can demonstrate that Addan has been the primary caregiver for the children, even while he and Damiyah were together, we can use that along with the fact that he had them fulltime the entire time after the divorce leading up to you guys' wedding. I think we can turn this around."

Addan was elated that Jessica was confident, but he didn't understand where his wife was coming from.

When they left Jessica's office, he wanted to question Nicole about what she said, but wrestled with whether he wanted to potentially start an argument.

After five minutes of traveling and not speaking but listening to the radio, Addan pressed the button to mute it. "What was that about back there?"

Nicole turned to him with wide eyes. "What was what?"

"The question you asked Jessica, about the mother usually being the one who gets the kids. Do you have a problem with the route I'm taking to get my children back?"

Nicole shook her head forcefully. "No, not at all. It's just..."

"Just what?" Addan's nostrils flared, and at that moment, he realized he was more upset at Nicole for her question than he originally thought he was. He softened. It wasn't her fault he was going through this. Nicole had been nothing but supportive the entire time. Maybe she only asked the question out of worry that things would be biased in Damiyah's favor. "Sorry for yelling, babe."

Nicole nodded, then stared out the window. "It's fine."

There was something in her tone as well as the deer-in-headlights look on her face ever since Addan asked what the issue was that tugged at the back of his mind, but Addan let it go. He already had drama with his ex-wife and children, he didn't want to add issues in his marriage on top of it.

Chapter 7

Nicole's return to her position as a medical assistant at one of the local clinics was a welcome distraction. Things had gotten tense between her and Addan when they left Jessica's office, and it was partially her fault. Nicole wanted to open up to her husband about what was troubling her but didn't know where to start.

Her relationship with Breon was the most traumatic situation of her life, and it seemed it would never end. While she was with him, she endured almost every type of abuse a woman could endure, and despite the fact that they ended their relationship over seven years ago, Breon had only just recently stopped taking her to court.

Nicole wrestled with whether she wanted to open up that can of worms and unload her burden onto her husband, but it turned out, Breon beat her to it.

She went to a nearby restaurant for take out on her lunch break and was eating at a picnic table at a nearby park. As her fingers found Addan's name in her contacts, his name and face flashed on her screen.

Nicole's heart pricked as she suspected this was not going to be a pleasant phone call. "Hello?"

Addan spoke in a low voice, but his tone was full of suspicion. "Let me ask you a question, Nicole."

From the way he said her name, Nicole knew this was about to be some drama. "What's going on?"

"I'm in the middle of a very interesting social media chat with your so-called ex-boyfriend, Breon."

Nicole's eyes widened with shock. "So-called? What do you mean?"

"I say so-called because per his screenshots, you two are still in contact with one another."

Nicole sputtered her next words. "Addan, what are you...?"

"Let me send you the evidence so you can see for yourself."

Nicole's heart dropped as she took in her husband's menacing tone. Her phone buzzed three times in her ear, but she did not want to look at the screenshots. Her eyes filled with tears. Why was Breon doing this? It seemed he would never let her go regardless of how much time passed since their relationship ended.

She reluctantly checked the messages and saw that sure enough, Breon had doctored several text conversations supposedly between him and her. The conversation sounded familiar, but Nicole knew for a fact that she hadn't texted Breon the things he was alleging.

"Look, Addan, I swear to you those are not real. The only thing I discuss with Breon is Briana, and I barely talk to him about her since she is sixteen and has her own phone."

Addan wasn't convinced, Nicole could tell. "You're alleging that Breon texted these messages to himself?"

Nicole knew how crazy it sounded, but she wouldn't put it past her ex. "Listen, I don't know who he was texting, but it wasn't me. Look at the language that is used. That's not even how I talk!"

Nicole's lunch was long-forgotten as she fumed in her seat.

"Yeah, well how does he know about my custody battle with Damiyah?"

"What?" Nicole's eyes popped open wider.

"There's no way he could have known about the case unless you told him, Nicole."

"Addan, I swear, I didn't... I don't know how he..." Her words came to a screeching halt as she realized exactly how Breon knew what was going on. "Wait a minute. Did Jessica already file the case?"

"What?"

"Did she file it with the courts yet, Addan?"

"Yes. She emailed me this morning. Why?"

The hairs on the back of her neck prickled. "That's how he found out. Breon must have checked public records, which means he's stalking me. Again."

Addan was silent as if he had been thrown for a loop. "Stalking you again? What do you mean? And that still doesn't explain the explicit messages, Nicole."

Now that Nicole had figured out Breon's scheme with the courts, she was determined to find where she had seen those texts before. Within a few moments of scrolling her timeline, it was as if God himself had intervened. "Got it!" she exclaimed.

"Got what?" was Addan's cross reply.

Nicole screenshotted the post and then sent it to Addan. "Go to that person's page and then read the post. That's where he got those messages. He must have photoshopped my name to the top of the text threads."

The line was silent for a moment as Addan did what Nicole instructed.

"What the hell...?" he said after a few moments.

"You see what I'm saying?" Nicole replied, her heart pounding in her ears.

"Why would he do something like this as if no one would ever find out?"

"Because that's how he is, Addan! He's crazy. I could go on for days about what that man put me through. I would never cheat on you, I promise, but I have a feeling I know why he popped up like this targeting you."

"Why?"

Nicole sighed. "I never told him we were getting married. He must have seen our wedding photos on social media."

Addan was silent for a moment. "You never told him? Why not?"

Nicole welled up again. "Because of stuff like this and worse. I was afraid he would show up to the ceremony or reception causing drama."

Addan's tone was now full of compassion. "Wow. I'm sorry, babe, for doubting you."

"You're good. I'm sorry too for not giving you the full story on my ex."

Addan made a sound. "Now that the door is open, it's time for you to let it all out. Tell me what I'm dealing with and what else I can expect from this man."

Nicole checked the time on her phone. "I can't get into it right now. I'm due back from lunch in less than ten minutes, but we'll talk soon, I promise."

"Okay, have a great day. Love you."

"Love you, too."

***

Nicole's fingers trembled as she dialed Breon's number the next day. The sound of the line ringing was a countdown to a confrontation she had hoped to avoid. As the call connected and Breon's gruff voice filled the line, Nicole's heart sank further.

"Why are you calling me, Nicole?" Breon's voice was as cold and unwelcoming as a winter storm.

"I need to know why you reached out to Addan," Nicole said, her voice steady despite the turmoil inside.

There was a brief silence before Breon scoffed. "Now you care what I do?"

Nicole bit back a retort. "You crossed a line, Breon. Dragging Addan into your games is unacceptable."

"Games?" Breon's voice rose in anger. "I wouldn't have to play games if you had the decency to tell me you were getting married!"

Nicole's patience was wearing thin. "My marriage is none of your business. You're engaged yourself, and you've been with countless other women since we split. Why would I need to tell you anything about my life?"

The line crackled with Breon's fury. Without another word, he ended the call, leaving Nicole staring at her phone in disbelief.

The silence that followed was heavy, and Nicole's mind raced. She had hoped that confronting Breon would bring some closure, but the abrupt end to their conversation only left her with a sinking feeling that this was far from over.

Nicole took a deep breath, trying to shake off the anxiety that clung to her like a second skin. She had to stay strong, for herself and for Addan. The past seven years had been a constant battle to keep Breon at a distance, and the last thing she wanted was to let him back into her life, even on the periphery.

She looked up, the clinic's walls offering little comfort. Patients came and went, each absorbed in their own world of concerns and ailments, oblivious to the drama unfolding in her life. Nicole mustered a smile for her next patient, but her mind was elsewhere, preparing for what she feared was just the beginning of a new chapter in her long history with Breon.

Chapter 8

Today was the day. Addan could not wait to get this court case over with so he could have his children safely back home with him where they belonged. Though two months had passed since Damiyah's stunt, Addan was still full of anger at the fact that she orchestrated such a sick scheme to rip Michael and Mikayah from the environment they were used to. It punched him in the gut because he felt like he hadn't protected them as a parent. Not that he thought Damiyah would hurt the children, but still. How could she take them like this?

Nicole had come to the proceedings for moral support, and it made Addan love her all the more. She had been his rock in this entire situation.

Jessica beamed at him, a confident gleam in her eyes as they stood on their side of the courtroom.

A few minutes later, Damiyah strode in. She was well-dressed in a navy blue suit, her hair and nails recently done, and six-inch heels adorning her feet, but all Addan felt for her was disgust. He couldn't believe he had been married to a woman who had it in her to do what she had done to him.

Light chatter broke out throughout the courtroom until Judge Tremblay, an African

American woman with stern features, entered the room.

"All rise," said the bailiff, then he announced the case.

Addan straightened in his seat. He hoped this would be open and shut and he could have his kids by the end of this hearing. Jessica had warned him that it might take more time than that, but Addan figured once she heard their side of the story, the judge would have no choice but to agree the kids needed to be with their father full time, which was the previous arrangement.

Jessica introduced herself at the judges' request, then Addan. After that, Judge Tremblay turned to Damiyah. "Ms. Nichols, do you have an attorney present today?"

Damiyah put her head down in what Addan knew to be fake embarrassment. "No judge, I don't. I couldn't afford one."

Judge Tremblay stared at Damiyah for a few moments, and Addan's stomach twisted as he saw a sense of compassion in her eyes. She faced straight ahead and said, "In that case, since Ms. Nichols does not have legal representation while Mr. Roberts does, I hereby appoint a special interest attorney to assist with this case for the benefit of the children involved. Mr. Roberts, Ms. Nichols, you will both meet with Sabrina Starr. She will decide after hearing both sides of the case about the best way to proceed. We will reconvene in three month's time. This hearing is adjourned."

Addan's head snapped in shock as the judge banged her gavel and asked for the next case. His mind was swimming. That was it? He looked over at Jessica. "What's happening?"

She gave him a forced smile. "Keep hope, Addan. We'll meet with Attorney Starr today, and she will instruct us on how to proceed."

Addan looked at the woman who would determine the fate of his children.

He could tell by the way she stared in his eyes that this would not go well for him.

Addan fought to keep hope alive as he followed Jessica out of the courtroom into another meeting room with Attorney Starr. Nicole followed as well, and she squeezed Addan's hand as they sat down.

Addan could feel frustration bubbling inside him like a cauldron on the verge of boiling over. He had walked into the courtroom with the expectation of justice, of being heard, and instead, he was met with a delay and a sense of helplessness that clawed at his chest. The anticipation of resolution had been replaced with the dread of extension and uncertainty.

As they entered the meeting room, the fluorescent lights buzzed overhead, casting a stark glow over the sterile space. Sabrina Starr, the court-appointed special interest attorney, was already seated at the table, a stack of papers in front of her. She looked up, her gaze piercing as if she was trying to read the very essence of his soul.

"Mr. Roberts," she began, her voice laced with a practiced neutrality that somehow felt cold, "I understand this is a difficult time, but I need to assess what's best for Michael and Mikayah. Please, tell me about your current living situation and your means to support your children."

As Addan answered her questions, he noticed that Sabrina's responses were curt, her pen barely scratching the surface of the paper as she took notes. It felt as though she was going through the motions, her mind already made up. When she turned her questions to Damiyah, her tone seemed to soften, her inquiries more in-depth, considerate.

The meeting dragged on, and with each passing minute, Addan's hope dimmed like the late afternoon light outside the window. He could tell his responses were being met with skepticism, that the narrative had been set against him, and he was just a player in a script written by others.

Jessica leaned in, her voice a whisper. "We've got this, Addan. Don't let this throw you off. We'll build on what we have and present a case that Sabrina can't ignore. It's about the kids, and I'll make sure she sees that."

Addan nodded, though his confidence wavered. He wanted to believe Jessica, to trust in the system he had put his faith in, but the walls of the meeting room seemed to close in on him, a physical manifestation of his growing despair.

Nicole's hand was a lifeline, her presence a silent vow of support. She didn't have to say a word; her determination spoke volumes. Addan knew he wasn't alone in this fight, and that realization steeled him against the tide of hopelessness threatening to sweep him away.

As they left the building, the sun dipping below the skyline, Addan looked up at the fading light. The road ahead was uncertain, the battle uphill, but with Nicole at his side and Jessica's unwavering commitment, he found the strength to face whatever came next. He had to—for Michael and Mikayah.

Chapter 9

Addan sat at his desk, the soft glow of the computer screen casting a pale light across the scattered papers and notes. His fingers flew across the keyboard as he compiled the evidence Jessica had asked for—proof of his stability and Damiyah's erratic patterns that had become the norm ever since their divorce. The emails and text messages formed a digital paper trail, showing not just his consistency and dedication to his children, but also Damiyah's frequent pleas for financial help.

He clicked send, and the documents were now on their way to Jessica. He knew this was strong; it had to be. His job had been his anchor for over a decade, and the home he had made was more than just a house—it was Michael and Mikayah's sanctuary, a place of memories and the only real stability they had ever known.

Jessica called him shortly after. "Addan, this is good. Really good. It shows a pattern, a history that we can present. It's tangible evidence of your commitment, not just to your job, but to providing a stable, loving home for your kids."

Her words were like a soothing medicine to Addan's frayed nerves, but the relief was short-lived. Later that day, the phone rang again, and this time it was Sabrina Starr on the line, her tone businesslike and unyielding.

"Mr. Roberts, I asked for references, not an email chain with their details. You should have provided their names, numbers, and email addresses separately. This is not a professional way to present such information."

Addan's grip tightened on the phone, his nerves unraveling. He had been trying to be efficient, to provide everything in one go. He hadn't anticipated this response.

"I apologize, Ms. Starr. I was trying to be thorough," he said, his voice steady despite the frustration simmering within.

"It's not the proper protocol," she snapped. "I won't be contacting your references if this is how you choose to provide their information."

The call ended abruptly, leaving Addan staring at the silent phone in disbelief. He felt a chill of foreboding, the sense that despite the evidence and Jessica's confidence, forces were aligning against him. He leaned back in his chair, the weight of the world pressing down on him.

But he couldn't succumb to despair. He thought of his children, their laughter, and their boundless energy. They were the reason he had to keep fighting, no matter the obstacles. On top of that, the evidence he just supplied Jessica should have amounted to a slam-dunk. He had held his job since before he met Damiyah, while she worked at twelve different companies during their thirteen-year marriage. The home he and Nicole resided in was purchased before he married Damiyah, another testament to his stability. That was without going into Damiyah's constant requests for money to help pay her rent and household bills, as well as the unfulfilled promises to pay him back. The more he thought about it, the more her actions were like a slap in the face.

Taking a deep breath, Addan picked up the phone and dialed Jessica's number. He relayed the conversation with Sabrina Starr, and though he couldn't see her, he could picture the determined set of Jessica's jaw.

"Don't worry, Addan. I'll handle it. This is just a hiccup. We'll provide the references again, the way she wants them," Jessica assured him. "We're going to keep pushing, and we won't let this derail us."

Addan hung up the phone, a mixture of appreciation and concern swirling within him. He looked out the window, where the sky was painted with the hues of dusk. He knew the road ahead would undoubtedly bring challenges, but as the stars began to twinkle into existence, he allowed himself a moment to believe that, like those distant lights, hope was not yet extinguished.

Chapter 10

Nicole's gaze was distant, her eyes unfocused as she sat on the edge of the bed she and Addan shared. The room was silent, except for the soft hum of the world outside, unaware of the storm brewing within her. Painful memories crept into her consciousness unbidden, painting the walls of her mind with scenes from a past she had tried to bury deep beneath layers of resilience and newfound strength.

She saw herself, years ago, laughing—a sound she scarcely recognized now—her hand in Jeremy's as they walked away from the little bistro that had become their spot. She and Jeremy had only dated a month, but it seemed that they were hitting it off nicely. Nicole enjoyed Jeremy's goofy nature—it was a stark contrast to Breon's years of abuse. The laughter died in her throat as headlights suddenly flared, an engine roared, and Breon's car mounted the curb in front of them. Jeremy's grip tightened before he was pulling away, running from the madness that was Breon, from the danger that she, unfortunately, could not escape so easily.

Nicole's life flashed before her eyes as Breon's headlights loomed before her. This was the end of her life. She could feel it.

The tires screeched, and Breon's voice cut through the night, laced with jealousy and the threat of violence. "You think you can just leave me for another man? I run your life, Nicole! When are you gonna realize that?" he hollered.

Once he saw that Nicole seemed to be okay, Jeremy disappeared into the night, and she was left standing alone, a figure frozen in the chaos of Breon's rage.

He slammed his driver's side door and stalked toward her, but thankfully, a nearby officer heard the commotion and came rushing over.

Nicole wished all the threats from Breon had ended with her safety.

Her heart raced in her chest as she snapped back to the present, her breaths coming in short, sharp gasps. The fear from that night was a living thing, clawing its way up her throat, choking her with the terror of history repeating itself.

She turned to look at Addan, who was standing in the doorway, his brow furrowed with concern. The stark contrast between Addan's steady, loving gaze and the fiery, possessive glares that Breon used to give her should have been reassuring. Yet, the fear that had taken root within her whispered insidious doubts, painting even Addan with the same brush as Breon.

"Is everything okay, Nicole?" Addan's voice was gentle, a stark contrast to the tumultuous waves of her flashback.

She nodded, not trusting her voice, not while the ghost of Breon's rage still echoed in her ears. Could she truly escape her past, or was it destined to taint everything good in her life? She loved Addan, but the love was entwined with fear—a fear that loving could once again lead to loss, that opening her heart could be an invitation to pain.

"Nicole?" Addan stepped closer, his presence warm and inviting yet unwittingly imposing.

She forced a smile, a brittle façade to mask the trembling of her soul. "I'm fine," she lied, the words tasting like ash in her mouth. But as he sat beside her, his hand finding hers, the steady beat of his heart seemed to call out to her own, offering a rhythm in the chaos, a possibility of a different ending than the one her fears scripted.

As they sat in silence, Nicole's gaze lingered on Addan. She wondered if Breon would ever truly leave her be or if the shadow cast by his wrath was a permanent sign of what was to come. The thought of losing Addan, of this being the beginning of the end, tightened its grip around her heart.

Yet, as Addan's thumb brushed softly against her skin, a wordless promise of support and understanding, Nicole dared to hope that perhaps this time, love would not be a prelude to disaster, but a bridge to a future where the past no longer held dominion over her heart.

Chapter 11

Addan was a bundle of nerves as he straightened out his suit jacket, adjusted his tie, and gave himself the umpteenth once-over in the full-length mirror that now adorned his and Nicole's bedroom. He looked like a great father and felt like one too, but Judge Tremblay would be the one to decide who received custody of the kids.

The last three months had been anxiety-inducing, to say the least.

Addan couldn't wrap his mind around the idea of only seeing his children on weekends when he had been with them every day of their lives from day one.

It wasn't fair.

Blinking back his emotions, he turned away from the mirror, breathing a silent prayer that Sabrina Starr would provide an unbiased opinion in court today.

None of his references had gotten back to him since he sent them over to her the professional way, and Addan didn't know if that was a good or bad sign.

He didn't want to pester anyone, but he also found it strange that none of them had reached out to him at least to tell him how the conversation went.

There wasn't time to dwell on that now, though. Now it was time to face the music.

Addan slowly descended the stairs and met Nicole in the middle of the living room. She was already dressed and ready, wearing a huge smile Addan knew was for his sake.

He hoped they would both be smiling by the end of the day.

"You ready?" Nicole asked as she leaned up to kiss his lips.

Addan obliged the gesture and forced a smile in her direction, but it didn't reach his eyes.

"Hey. It will be okay," Nicole encouraged in a softer tone.

Addan nodded and swallowed.

They exited the house, and before they left, Addan noted the silence. Was this how it would always be? For as long as he could remember, his home had been full of laughter, pattering feet, TV's and music blasting at top volume, and arguments over toys and games. How could it all be over because of Damiyah's selfish actions?

Addan was so lost in thought that he hadn't noticed Nicole had taken his car key from his hand. It wasn't until he felt her gently guiding him toward the passenger seat of his car that he snapped out of it.

"Sorry," he said, speaking for the first time that morning.

"Don't worry," she encouraged. "I know your mind is running a mile a minute, but hopefully by the end of today we will have solid answers about where this is going."

Addan nodded and stepped into his seat, clicking his seatbelt as Nicole entered the driver's side door and shut it, then cranked up the engine.

Soft gospel music played from Addan's playlist as soon as his phone connected to the Bluetooth.

Addan and Nicole listened in silence as they traveled. By the time they arrived at the courthouse, Addan was in better spirits. He allowed himself to relax, reasoning that whatever happened today was in God's hands. He had prepared to the best of his ability with Jessica, supplied all the necessary evidence, and answered every question Sabrina Starr shot his way.

He tensed when his eyes caught Sabrina resting a hand on Damiyah's elbow as the two women shared a laugh, but Addan didn't allow his thoughts to sway in a negative direction. At the same time, for a special interest attorney who was supposed to be unbiased, Sabrina was quite chummy with his ex-wife.

The more Addan tried to keep his thoughts neutral, the more the sight of what was happening before him rubbed him the wrong way. As he was about to walk over and say something, Jessica stepped into his path wearing her customary determined smile.

"Ready to win this thing?" Her grin widened.

He wanted to spit out how he really felt, but Addan reasoned that would be a slap in Jessica's face. She had worked alongside him through this whole journey. He wouldn't take that from her.

They strode into the courtroom together and took their seats, waiting for the hearing to begin.

Now that they were inside the courtroom, Sabrina sat at a distance from Damiyah, and the two women barely shared eye contact.

Addan's fists balled at his sides. A gloomy feeling swept over him, and he couldn't force it down.

"All rise," the bailiff said, promptly on time.

Addan stood with everyone else, but as soon as he reached his full height, his heart sank to the floor.

Judge Tremblay entered the room and took her seat wearing the same stern expression she wore the first time Addan saw her.

Once the case was announced, Jessica attempted to speak, but Judge Tremblay didn't allow it.

"I have decided to hear solely from Attorney Starr on this case as the court has appointed her to provide an unbiased opinion."

"But, Judge—" Jessica stammered and gave Addan a look like a deer caught in headlights.

"I have made my decision, Counselor."

Jessica had no choice but to back down.

Addan had a feeling how this was going to go but tried his best to hold out hope.

"Please, Lord," he whispered under his breath, "I'm praying for a miracle."

Nicole looked at him as if asking what he had just said, but Addan didn't respond.

Chapter 12

Addan exited the courtroom on shaky legs. It was as if the entire world had stopped rotating. Everything in his life stood still. His body was filled with shock. His mind flooded with white noise.

Nicole was standing next to him saying something, but Addan couldn't make out the words, nor could he turn his head to face her.

It was as if his limbs held a mind of their own as Judge Tremblay's voice broke through the white noise, and her words sounded in his ears.

"I hereby declare that primary custody shall be awarded to Ms. Nichols. Mr. Roberts, you will be allowed to see the children on weekends, and they shall stay with you during their summer breaks..."

He lost.

Addan lost his kids.

Michael and Mikayah, his pride and joy. His son and daughter. He was the first to hold them both the day they were born. So tiny and fragile in his hands, and now a woman who didn't know him from a brick in the wall relied on the biased opinion of a so-called special interest attorney to strip them from his loving arms.

Sabrina Starr had a special interest, alright.

An interest in serving mothers only.

Addan hated the narrative that was often spun about Black fathers. He had never once neglected or abandoned his kids. He was easily the more involved parent all their lives. Every time they needed something, he supplied it. Every time they fell and skinned a knee, he was the one there mending it and kissing away the pain.

When they had events at school, Addan was in the stands cheering them on amongst a sea of other parents. PTO meetings, he was the voice of reason, coming up with all the hottest ideas to raise money for the betterment of the kids.

And it all meant nothing because the courts always sided with the mother.

Damiyah had given him a smug smile at first after the verdict was read, but once she saw his face, her expression changed. It was as if her air of victory was short lived, and she suddenly realized this was not a game for Addan.

For Addan, his kids were his life. He dedicated his time, money, and efforts to make sure they had the best lives, better lives than he had growing up. Damiyah knew this. She knew how much he loved those kids.

And now he could only see them on the weekends, all because Damiyah got mad at the fact that he was married?

When she dated man after man after their divorce, Addan said nothing. When she changed her mind and said she wanted to rekindle their bond, Addan stepped forward and gave it his best shot. As soon as he did, Damiyah stepped back as if she had lost interest and let him do all the work.

After he grew tired of feeling like he was forcing something that was no longer there, Addan gave up and pursued other options.

It just so happened that Nicole was the first woman he dated, and things turned serious quickly. When Addan and Nicole talked about marriage, Addan immediately informed Damiyah. Admittedly, she hung up the phone on him when she heard the news, but Addan didn't think much of it because she acted like she wasn't interested in him anyway and had already dated several other men before he pursued any other woman.

Now that he had his happiness, she became the source of his pain.

Where did he go from here?

How could he survive without his children?

"Baby?" Nicole's voice broke Addan from his thoughts. He jerked back to attention and realized they were still standing on the courthouse steps, and a raindrop had just fallen on the top of his head.

He turned to face his wife, and her eyes were brimming with tears. "We have to go home now. Okay?"

Addan wordlessly nodded and followed her.

He knew Nicole felt his pain, but he couldn't find the words to thank her for being there for him. In fact, he couldn't think of any words at all at the moment.

Jessica's voice carried in the wind as they entered the car, but Addan slammed the passenger's side door and didn't look back.

Chapter 13

Now that the damage was done to her husband, Nicole struggled to figure out how they were supposed to pick up the pieces. She knew she was supposed to say something, do something to make it better, but she couldn't think of anything.

If the shoe was on the other foot and Breon had somehow managed to take Briana from Nicole, she would be ready for war.

It was one thing to lie, cheat, hit, and hurt her in every way possible, but all hell would break loose if Breon ever tried to mess with her child.

Speaking of Breon, his name flashed across Nicole's phone screen. Receiving a text message from him caused an instant migraine.

What, had he followed the case and found out Addan lost his kids? Was he texting to gloat about what happened?

Nicole didn't feel like dealing with Breon's mess today. She ignored the message.

"Mom?" Briana said, when Nicole and Addan entered the house.

Nicole was taken aback at the sight of her daughter, first because she wasn't supposed to be home yet from school, and two, because of the bruise on the left side of her face.

Nicole snapped out of the funk she was in over Addan's situation and rushed over to her daughter.

"Baby, what's wrong? What happened?" Nicole gently touched the area where the bruise was, and her heart panged, then twisted. Rage immediately coursed through her as wild thoughts ran through her mind. Whoever had done this was going to pay.

"I fell," Briana said, then sniffled and looked down.

That was a lie, but the way her daughter said it made Nicole pause. "What do you mean, you fell, baby?" she said in the gentlest voice she could muster.

Nicole turned back to look at Addan, and he was studying their interaction. His face contorted in pain, then he headed upstairs without a word.

Nicole would have to soothe him later. For now, her daughter needed her attention.

"Briana?" she said, when her daughter hadn't spoken for over a minute.

Briana finally raised her head, eyes full of tears. "The other girls don't like me."

Those words were like a punch in the gut. Questions immediately flooded Nicole's brain. Briana had always been somewhat of a loner, but Nicole never heard her complain about not having friends. She mentioned a girl she did homework with sometimes, so Nicole figured Briana was the type to keep her circle small. She never would have guessed her daughter was being bullied.

"What do you mean they don't like you? What happened?" Nicole guided Briana to the couch. They sat, and Briana pulled her feet up, wrapping her arms around her knees. She shrugged but didn't offer anything further.

"Did something happen today at school?" Nicole asked. Obviously, it had since her daughter was home early, but Nicole was trying to give her space to tell the story her own way.

Briana nodded. "Kate got mad that I wouldn't let her copy my assignment. She threatened to fight me during gym class, but I stayed close to the teacher. Then when it was over..." A tear rolled down Briana's cheek. "I didn't realize Ashley was going to help her get to me. I was trying to get away from Kate, and Ashley pushed me down the stairs."

Nicole bristled as she gasped. "Pushed you down the stairs!"

Briana didn't respond.

"Briana, are you hurt anywhere else? What did the principal say? Nobody called me and said anything!" Nicole's nostrils flared. She was so upset. Why hadn't anyone notified her about what happened to her daughter?

"I didn't tell," Briana said and pulled her knees tighter, like she was trying to curl into a ball and disappear.

Something snapped within Nicole. "I'm going to your school." She stood from the couch and yanked her purse from the end table. School didn't let out for another hour so that was plenty of time.

"No, Mom!" Briana's eyes widened in fear as she pleaded. "You can't do that. If they think I'm a snitch..."

"It's not snitching. That was assault, and in some courts, they would call it attempted murder. I am not going to let these girls put their hands on you, Briana."

"But, Mom, if you tell on them, things will only get worse for me!"

Briana was practically hysterical, her eyes bulging as she gripped Nicole's arms with the strength of a grown woman.

Where had Nicole gone wrong? How had she not seen the signs of what her daughter was going through? Nicole was happy that Briana trusted her enough to share what happened, but now she felt conflicted. If she went to the school and confronted the teachers, would her daughter ever share anything again? What if things did get worse? What if Briana internalized their actions? What if she...?

Nicole focused on her daughter. "Are you hurt anywhere else?"

Briana forcefully shook her head. "No, just my face. I'm fine."

"Lift your shirt."

Briana did as Nicole instructed, and Nicole gently pressed her hands against different parts of her body trying to ensure her daughter wasn't seriously injured.

After Briana's constant assurance that no part of her body hurt, Nicole still wasn't satisfied. "How did only your face get bruised?"

Briana swallowed. "That happened after."

Nicole stared at her daughter. "What do you mean? Something happened after they pushed you down the stairs?"

Briana nodded. "I only fell down a few stairs, and when Kate and Ashley saw they didn't hurt me like they wanted to, they followed me. I tried to make it to my next class, but they surrounded me, and other girls were on their side too. I told Kate to leave me alone and that's when she punched me."

"Did you hit her back?"

Briana shook her head and looked down. "I just wanted them to go away, but the boys got in it, and they all kept trying to egg on a fight. I broke through the crowd and left school. I came here."

"And no teachers saw any of this?"

Briana shrugged. "They barely pay attention to what goes on."

That was a serious problem.

"Briana, if that girl ever puts her hands on you again, you hit her back. Hear me?"

Briana nodded, but it was a half-hearted gesture. Nicole knew she wouldn't do it.

Now there was another problem to add to the pile as Nicole had to figure out how to handle Briana's situations while comforting Addan about his children.

**

The weekend couldn't come soon enough.

It was Breon's weekend to take Briana, and Nicole didn't want her to go at first because she was still trying to keep an ear out for the bullying situation, but Briana insisted so she couldn't say no. Briana was a daddy's girl, and despite Nicole's resentment toward Breon, she would not take her daughter from her father.

Addan wanted to take his kids out to the arcade for a few hours. Since Briana was gone with Breon, Nicole asked to tag along, but Addan said he wanted to be alone with them. Nicole understood. Her husband was going through a traumatic experience and trying to pick up the pieces.

She would let him have his time.

Since everyone was gone, Nicole had the house to herself. She flipped on the TV and searched for one of her shows so she could binge watch it and catch up.

She was halfway through the episode when Breon's name and number flashed across her phone screen. Nicole sucked her teeth. She did not want to talk to him, but it could have been about Briana, so she answered.

"Hello?"

"Oh, now you answer your phone."

Breon was already irritating her, and the conversation had barely started.

"What is it, Breon?"

"I texted you the other day, but since you didn't answer, I decided to take matters into my own hands."

Nicole straightened in her seat. "What do you mean, take matters into your own hands?"

"You should have answered my text. Briana's about to get a tattoo."

Nicole's blood boiled. "She what? No, she is not getting a tattoo, Breon!"

"Yes, she is. If she wants one, I'm going to get it for her."

"Put my daughter on the phone."

"She's our daughter, Nicole, and no."

"Do it now, Breon!" Nicole's voice was a thunderous demand, her heart pounding in her chest like a drumbeat.

Breon's laughter crackled through the line, a sound of pure, undiluted scorn. "You're not in control here, Nicole. And you can't stop what's already happening."

Nicole's fingers danced furiously across her phone, trying to initiate a three-way call to Briana. The call rang, then rang some more, before going to voicemail. She cursed under her breath, the taste of fear mingling with anger on her tongue. Why wasn't Briana answering? She had never been a rebellious girl. Nicole sent her a text, hoping she would answer that.

Breon's voice was relentless, a steady stream of venom. "She's growing up, Nicole. She wants to express herself, and a tattoo is what she wants."

"She's a child, Breon! You can't make that decision for her!" Nicole's shout was sharp enough to slice through the tension, but it did nothing to sway Breon.

Nicole stared at the text thread between herself and her daughter, but there was no sign Briana had seen the message. That didn't make sense. Briana always had her phone with her, just like any other teenager.

As if Breon heard her thoughts, he said, "Texting her won't help. I have her phone."

"Why do you have her phone, Breon? Where is she? You better not have her up in some tattoo parlor now!" The digital map on Nicole's screen showed no location for Briana; her settings were private, a black hole in the web of satellite precision. Nicole's voice was a whip, cracking through the air. "Where are you? Tell me where you are right now!"

Breon was clearly enjoying his moment. "A father can do a lot of things, Nicole. Maybe you'd know that if you weren't so busy playing the martyr."

Nicole's thoughts were a blur of motion. She fired up her browser, her search history becoming a frantic stream of legal inquiries, but it returned an abyss of uncertainty. He couldn't do this legally, could he? Unfortunately, the answer didn't come to her automatically.

Her blood pressure continued to rise as Breon's taunts antagonized her.

Just as she was about to leave the house and get in her car to search for them, he dropped the act.

"Relax, Nicole. I haven't made any appointments. Yet." His words slithered into her ear; a snake clothed in revelation.

Nicole stared at her phone in shock. As the adrenaline faded, her racing heart slowed, and the fog lifted from her mind. It was all a ruse, a game, a way for Breon to claw into her life and stir the pot of her anxieties. He was playing his old games, dealing his cards of chaos.

"What the hell is wrong with you?" she uttered. "Did you really just call me and say all that to play games?"

"No, I called you to discuss our daughter."

"Where is Briana, Breon?"

"Relax, she's coming to our table now. She had to use the bathroom. We're at a restaurant."

Nicole was so furious she hung up the phone.

A few seconds later, Briana responded to her frantic text, asking what was going on and why she asked where she was.

Nicole felt like a fool as she responded. *Just checking up on you. What's this I hear about you wanting a tattoo?*

Nicole braced herself for her daughter's response then felt like an even bigger fool when she responded. *I don't want a tattoo. Dad and I talked about it, but I only told him I liked his tattoo, not that I wanted one of my own.*

Sooner or later, Nicole would have to find a way to stop Breon's antics for good.

Chapter 14

Addan had looked forward to this weekend all week, but now that it was here, it was bittersweet. Michael was overjoyed to see him, but Mikayah acted as if she didn't want to be bothered. Damiyah had to be poisoning her mind.

Another dagger to his heart.

How could the woman turn so cruel over nothing? It wasn't like Nicole was a bad woman. Damiyah had to know that Addan would never marry someone who would cause harm to his children.

Addan's mind went to Nicole and her daughter, Briana. It seemed that his wife was dealing with her own issues now that he was entangled in his. Addan felt like a horrible husband for letting Nicole deal with Briana's bullying incident by herself. He should have been there for her as a support, especially since she had supported him with his case, but he dropped the ball.

His mind was so consumed with the new reality of only seeing his kids on weekends and summers that he wasn't able to do anything for her.

Addan made it a point to have a conversation with Nicole later that night. Maybe they could sign Briana up for martial arts or boxing lessons.

He returned his attention to his children. Michael and Mikayah were playing a heated racing game against each other, and their trash talk was hilarious. Normally, Addan Jr. would be with them, but Addan sent Niya a text briefly explaining his situation and she sent Addan Jr. to her parents' house for the weekend.

Addan whipped out his phone to record the moment, but when Mikayah turned back and saw what he was doing, she stopped the game.

"Hey, what are you doing?" Michael said as his car soared past hers. He faced his sister as she stepped away from the game and sat on a nearby stool.

Michael's car crossed the finish line, then he looked from his dad to his sister. "Come on, Mikayah. It's not true what Mommy said."

Addan's ears pricked at those words. "What do you mean, what Mommy said?"

Michael shrugged, still staring at his sister. "Nothing."

Addan wanted to press it, especially since it seemed that his prior concern about Damiyah poisoning his kids' minds was well founded, but he didn't. That would only cause more drama.

"How about some pizza?" he suggested, redirecting the conversation instead.

"Yes!" Michael said, while Mikayah stared off into the distance.

"We can get ice cream afterward..." Addan said, giving her a playful smile and praying she bit the bait. Addan's daughter loved ice cream.

That seemed to do the trick. Mikayah lightened up as they went to the pizza station and placed their orders.

After eating, they played a few more games then headed to the ice cream spot on the way home. Addan made sure to order Nicole's favorite ice cream to go.

Now that things seemed to be going smoother with the kids, Addan felt bad for not taking Nicole up on her offer to tag along. It would have been the perfect opportunity for her and Mikayah to bond.

The rest of the evening went well, but Addan noticed that Michael warmed up to Nicole immediately, while Mikayah barely said a word to her. When they did speak, Mikayah's answers were short like she only responded to be polite.

This was a problem.

Addan would have to find a way to get through to his daughter, but it would likely be tough if Damiyah was in her ear throughout the week.

The next day was church, and they went together as a family.

Addan enjoyed the service, and the kids seemed to be in good spirits. That was, until one of the deacons made a comment. "Wow, I never noticed how you two favor!" He was looking back and forth between Mikayah and Nicole.

Now that he mentioned it, Addan saw the resemblance too. Nicole smiled, but before she could say a word, Mikayah cut in with a biting response. "I look nothing like that woman. She is not my mother."

The deacon's eyes widened as Addan reprimanded his daughter. "Mikayah! What's gotten into you? You apologize to Deacon Brown and Nicole right now."

Mikayah put her head down. "Sorry, Deacon Brown."

Deacon Brown nodded as if he understood he had just opened a can of worms. "You all have a blessed Sunday." He walked away.

Addan's expression hardened as he focused on his daughter. "Mikayah, I didn't hear you apologize to Nicole."

Mikayah remained silent; her features etched in defiance.

"Let's go to the car," Nicole said, her face flushed in hurt and embarrassment.

Addan wasn't having that, but it was a delicate situation, so he would have to talk to his daughter alone.

They ordered take out on the way home then ate together as a family when they arrived at the house.

Once everyone was settled, Addan went to Mikayah's room. Her door was closed, and she was watching TV, from the sounds of it.

"Yes?" she asked when he knocked.

"Can I come in?"

A few moments passed before her tone changed to slight annoyance. "Come in."

Addan opened the door and closed it behind him, approaching his daughter, who was sitting on her bed. "How are you doing?"

Mikayah continued to stare at the screen. "I'm fine."

"What was that comment about earlier? Why did you speak about Nicole in that way?"

Mikaya's jaw was set in stone. "She's not my mother."

"No, she's not, but I don't understand why you had to say it the way you did. Did you know Nicole's feelings were hurt by your comment?"

Mikayah shrugged. "So?"

"Mikayah!" Addan's tone was stern now. "You need to fix your attitude."

She finally faced him. "Or what, Daddy? You gonna leave us completely? Mommy already told us you were leaving us for Nicole and her daughter. That's why we live with her now."

Addan's eyes widened in shock. "What? Mikayah, that's not true!"

"Then why do we only see you on the weekend, huh? Why do we have to go to that new school? You don't love us anymore!"

Her tiny heart was broken, and there wasn't a thing Addan could do to fix it. He wrapped his arms around his daughter as tears streamed down her face.

There were a number of things he wanted to say and do to Damiyah, because now she had gone too far, but Addan felt powerless. If he said anything bad about her mother, Addan would be bringing his kids into their drama. He had to handle this the right way, but he didn't know what the right way was.

"Listen to me," he said, pulling back to look in his daughter's eyes. "I will never stop loving you. You are my pride and joy and the apple of my eye. Your mother and I may not be together anymore, but no one will ever replace you or Michael for me. Do you believe that?"

Mikayah seemed to take in his words as she nodded, but Addan sensed in his heart that the problems weren't over.

Chapter 15

When Addan went to Mikayah's room to talk to her about the incident that happened earlier, Nicole was left alone with her thoughts.

It seemed that life was better before she married Addan.

Yes, things were lonely being a single woman raising a daughter while dodging a treacherous and manipulative ex, but when she added Addan to the mix, his problems came with him.

Addan was a wonderful husband and father, but his ex-wife Damiyah seemed just as hellbent on destroying Addan as Breon was at destroying her. Why wouldn't those two just knock it off? Breon was consumed with Nicole's marriage with Addan, yet he was engaged to a whole other woman. Nicole never had a problem with that. If any woman was willing to take him off her hands, she welcomed it.

And Addan had said things with Damiyah were great before Nicole came around. She dated other men and had even grown serious with one of them. Addan powered through it, reasoning that at some point, they both would move on, but the minute he tried to move on, that was when the problems came.

It wasn't fair.

All Nicole and Addan wanted to do was be happy. Raise their kids and love them to the best of their abilities, while building a life with each other.

But after that recent incident with Breon, Nicole knew more was coming. She didn't like to think of her past, but sometimes memories broke through.

After Nicole had finally mustered the strength to break up with him, Breon refused to back down, resolving to make her life a living hell. Breon's pursuit was relentless. Nicole had moved to a new apartment to get away from the man, but he kept showing up everywhere she went: her job, Briana's school parking lot, and when she went out with friends. The restraining order was supposed to be her shield, but he turned it into a weapon, an excuse to draw closer, close enough to feel his breath on the back of her neck. Nicole had never heard of someone appealing a restraining order, but Breon did it, then he twisted the dagger by moving next door to her new apartment.

After that came the flurry of court cases. They were a carousel of madness, spinning her round and round until the world blurred. Each summons was a paper cut, trivial in isolation but collectively a hemorrhage of her spirit. In the years since Nicole and Breon's breakup, Breon had taken her to court over thirty times, just because he could. Nicole had seen the inside of courtrooms so much that she had PTSD. She barely wanted to check the mail because it always seemed that Breon had constructed a new reason to take her to court. Whether it was for changing the time of his pickup, to changing the date, to revising the location, the cases racked up. Then came the silly lawsuits, the most prominent of which being his accusation that Nicole had stolen his identity and used it to order a cable service in his name. The case was thrown out, but another one came after it, then another. Things got so bad that Nicole and Briana were homeless at one point, all because Breon kept taking her to court, and she couldn't afford to keep up with him. Nicole learned the law to the point where she no longer needed to hire an attorney. Once she started representing herself and winning, the court cases slowed down. Then they stopped altogether a year before Nicole met Addan. She figured Breon had moved on.

But he hadn't. Apparently, he had been waiting for a new opportunity to torment her.

The tattoo incident was not the beginning, nor would it be the end. It was just another rotation of the carousel, another dizzying loop.

Nicole closed her eyes, a vain attempt to barricade her mind from the onslaught of the past, but the images were there, imprinted on the insides of her eyelids, playing like a silent movie to an audience of one.

The sound of her own breathing was a metronome in the quiet, each inhale a measure of her resolve, each exhale a release of her fears. When would it ever end? The question was a weight, but also a beacon. She couldn't control Breon's actions, nor Damiyah's vendetta against Addan, but she could steer her own ship through the storm.

Nicole's eyes snapped open, a new determination kindling within them. The past may have written some of her story, but the pen was now in her hand. It was time to chart a new course, to navigate through their various situations the best way she knew how.

She would start with a plan, a strategy to counter Breon's next move. No more would she be the defendant in his twisted court; it was time to take the gavel. With Addan by her side, they would face the storm together, an unbreakable front against the winds of their adversaries.

Nicole rose from the couch; her body weary, but her spirit unwavering. The road ahead was uncertain, but one thing was crystal clear: she had survived Breon's attempts before, and she would do so again.

Chapter 16

When the next weekend rolled around, Addan had a plan. The first weekend was spent with mostly him and the kids, but he had to find a way to foster a bond between Nicole and Mikayah. The perfect idea came to mind: a family photo.

With a family photo, all the kids could be included, plus him and Nicole. Maybe that would help soothe Mikayah's psyche about the idea of her father having a new wife and stepdaughter.

Addan also hoped it would be an opportunity for the girls to bond. Briana was older than Mikayah, being sixteen to Mikayah's thirteen, but they seemed to get along up to this point. Mikayah's main problem seemed to be with Nicole.

Thinking about what Mikayah said Damiyah told her and Michael made Addan's blood boil. She wasn't playing fair by trying to drive a wedge between him and his kids.

He and Nicole seemed to be getting along fine, but Addan couldn't help but to feel like if things didn't smooth out soon, it would cause strain in their marriage. His other ex wife, Niya, had never done anything like what Damiyah was doing.

Addan and Damiyah had their problems, which inevitably led them to divorce, but before their issues, they had years of bliss. The first few years of Michael and Mikayah's lives were filled with precious memories.

Addan wanted to build precious memories with Nicole, but it seemed their problems started the day after they said, "I do."

Was Nicole thinking the same thing? They hadn't discussed the elephant in the room. Addan hoped Nicole wasn't regretting marrying him.

The kids were busy getting dressed in their rooms, and Nicole was in the shower. Addan was already ready. He fixed his tie and stared at his reflection in the mirror, hoping today would be a good day.

"Daddy?" Addan turned to see Michael standing in the doorway holding his tie. "Can you help me?"

"Sure, son." Michael walked into the room and Addan slowly showed him how to tie it, explaining the steps as he went. When he finished, Michael looked confused but grateful. "Do you think you'll be able to do that yourself next time?" Addan teased.

Michael gave him a bashful smile, and it reminded Addan of one of the pictures his mom had in her photo album. Addan had the album in one of the hallway closets. He inherited it when his mother passed.

He would have to show Michael the picture later. He was sure his son would get a kick out of seeing what his father looked like decades ago.

Nicole exited the bathroom at that moment and walked toward the bedroom wearing her bathrobe. She gave Addan and Michael a warm smile.

"Come on, kiddo," Addan urged, and he and Michael headed out of the room and downstairs to the living room to watch TV before they left.

Briana and Addan Jr. were already downstairs, dressed, and ready, and Addan felt bad because he had forgotten about Briana.

"Hey Briana," Addan said.

She looked up from her cell phone and gave him a shy smile. "Hey."

Addan flipped on the TV, then gestured to hand the remote to Addan Jr. He passed, so Addan handed Michael the remote. He turned it to some anime channel and started excitedly explaining the characters to his older brother and father. Addan was more excited at the glee in his son's eyes than he was at the story he was telling.

Nicole came downstairs after about twenty minutes. The only person left was Mikayah.

"Don't you two look handsome!" Nicole said, and Addan inhaled the scent of her perfume as she bent down to give him a kiss before sitting next to him on the couch. That brief moment caused him to swell with arousal, but now wasn't the time for that. He would have plenty of time to undress his wife later.

Fifteen minutes later, Mikayah slowly thumped down the stairs, then she stopped short halfway down, looking over the banister with disgust.

"We're all wearing the same dress?"

Nicole stood. "Yes, I thought it would be cute. Why?"

Mikayah stiffened. "I don't want to look like you."

Nicole was hurt, Addan could tell, but she held it together. "Actually, Mikayah, your dress is different from mine. See? It's more like Briana's." Nicole was pleading with her eyes for Mikayah's approval, and Addan didn't like it. He knew his daughter was acting out because of her mother, but it gave her no right to continually disrespect his wife.

Mikayah crossed her arms. "I'm changing my dress, or I'm not going."

Addan stood. "You will not change your dress, and you will go. Come downstairs. Now."

Mikayah's eyes pooled at the sternness of her father's tone. "Daddy, why do I have to?"

"Because we're a family, that's why."

"But she's not my family..."

"Mikayah, you have one more time."

Father and daughter stared each other down, neither of them willing to budge.

"Ten seconds," Addan said.

Five seconds later, Mikayah stomped the rest of the way down the stairs.

Needless to say, everyone wasn't smiling in the family photos.

On the way home from the photo outing, Addan texted Damiyah.

I feel like you, Nicole, and I need to have a conversation. Would you be open to a Zoom meeting?

When they arrived at the house, Damiyah hadn't responded yet.

A few hours later, still no reply.

Addan's mind became consumed with how to fix the issue before it went too far. Sooner or later, something had to give.

Chapter 17

Later that night, after the kids were in their rooms, Addan took his wife's hands.

"Hey, how are you feeling?" He stared down into her eyes.

Nicole peered up at him. "Like I'm dealing with multiple ticking time-bombs that are waiting to explode."

Addan nodded, figuring as much. His wife was just as stressed as he was. "How about we pray?" he suggested.

Nicole stared at him, then nodded, bowing her head.

"Father, we come to you on behalf of our family. You know our situation, Lord. Nicole and I just got married, but it seems our problems came as soon as we tied the knot. Lord, we believe you are the one who brought us together, but all these situations are taxing us. Please work out the situation with Briana at school. Lord, help her to find some friends and touch the hearts of the girls who seem to want to cause her harm. Let not a hair on her head be touched and give my wife the wisdom to know what to say and do."

Addan paused, becoming overwhelmed with emotion about all that was going on, and Nicole cut in.

"Father, we also ask that you rebuke the enemy who is trying to cause a separation between Addan and his children. We pray that Mikayah understands that her father loves her, and he would never try to replace her as his daughter."

Addan jumped back in. "And Lord we ask that you work out the situations between Mikayah and Nicole as well as me, Nicole, and Damiyah. This whole family needs your touch. Lord, we ask that you help us navigate these murky waters of broken relationships and send healing and reconciliation for our hearts and minds. Help us to work together as a blended family and for Damiyah to be at peace with the fact that I have moved on. All these things we ask in Jesus' name."

As husband and wife, Addan and Nicole said, "Amen" together.

After the prayer, Addan felt lighter, as if God had heard him and that things were going to turn around.

The next morning, it seemed his suspicions were confirmed. Damiyah responded to his text message.

Sure, that's fine. Just let me know the day and time.

Addan's heart leapt with joy. He immediately shared the news with Nicole, and she seemed excited too. Maybe if things smoothed out between the three of them, Damiyah would agree to a different custody agreement. Addan still had his heart on his kids living back with him full time.

He wouldn't mention it during this first discussion, though.

Hopefully things would work out.

Chapter 18

Although things seemed to be turning around for Addan's situation, Nicole couldn't shake the feeling that her own problems were about to get worse. She kept having flashbacks of her and Breon's relationship and didn't know why.

Was God trying to warn her that her ex was planning something?

Nicole hoped not, because Mikayah's rebellion and Briana's bullying situation were already enough, not to mention the looming conversation with Damiyah.

Nicole remembered the brief social media encounter she had with a man she was interested in dating a year after she ended things with Breon.

She met the man in a Christian singles group, and after they commented on a few of each other's posts, he sent her a friend request.

Nicole excitedly accepted but didn't DM him because she wanted him to come to her. After a day or two, he started liking her pictures and posts.

Nicole returned the favor by doing the same thing on his profile.

After a week of their back and forth semi-flirting, Nicole was pleasantly surprised to see that not only had he hearted one of her posts, but he commented as well, agreeing with her opinion.

The post was a meme about relationships and moving on. The man had commented that the words rang true and that he was looking for a lovely lady to move on with. *How about you, Nicole?* He had written. *Are you looking for a man to move on with, or is a brother getting his hopes up for nothing?*

Nicole blushed at how bold and forward he was. The man was openly declaring his interest, which dramatically reduced the chances that he was the type to play games.

She fixed her fingers to send him a flirty reply indicating that she was indeed interested, but before she could, a reply popped up on her screen underneath the man's comment. Someone named Troy Mathis said, *Chill bruh. Trust me, you don't wanna go that route. She gets around.*

Nicole clapped a hand over her mouth.

Excuse me? her suitor responded.

I'm serious, Troy wrote back. *She burned me a few months ago. Get tested if you already tapped that.*

Mortified wasn't the word.

Nicole immediately knew the man behind "Troy's" profile was Breon.

She deleted the post, then immediately inboxed the man she had been flirting with to salvage her reputation. *Hey,* she texted. *Please don't take that man's words seriously. I have never dated anyone named Troy. That's my ex, Breon. He's the one behind that profile.*

Unfortunately, her suitor wasn't interested in hearing her explanation.

Nicole, I'm sorry we wasted each other's time. I was under the impression you didn't have any man in your life. You say he's your ex, but he has to be recent if he's still on you like this. I'm sorry, but I'm no longer interested.

Nicole wanted to write back and say she and Breon had ended things over a year ago, but her instincts told her that wouldn't matter. He was already turned off, which meant Breon had succeeded yet again at ruining something in her life.

Breon continued that pattern of behavior every time she tried to talk to a new man, until it got to the point where Nicole gave up on relationships altogether.

It seemed she could never be happy if Breon was around.

Meanwhile, he had multiple extended relationships after Nicole, and she never said a word about it.

When she finally became fed up and tried a Christian dating app, Nicole was at her wits end. She was about to give up on that too, especially when she saw Breon's profile on the site, even though he was engaged.

But she persisted on the app and met Addan, then they grew serious and got married.

As soon as that happened, here Breon came again.

Had she made a mistake?

Chapter 19

Addan could not wait for the Zoom meeting.

The more he looked forward to it, the more he wished he had suggested it earlier. Maybe if he, Damiyah, and Nicole had been engaged in regular conversations before he and Nicole got married, things would have never turned out the way they did.

"Oh well, better late than never," he mused, and headed downstairs to the living room with his laptop. When he got there, Nicole wasn't there.

"Nicole?" he called out, swearing he heard her down here watching TV a few moments ago.

"I'm in the kitchen!" she responded. "Let's do the call in here."

"Okay." Addan whistled as he carried his laptop and charger to the kitchen to begin the call. His heart pounded with every step, but he had a feeling it would turn out fine and they would reach a common understanding. Then, maybe later he and Damiyah could discuss a revised custody agreement for the kids.

Addan entered the kitchen to see Nicole sitting at the table looking nervous. He pulled up a seat next to her and opened the laptop screen, then plugged his charger into a nearby outlet before pressing the other end into the laptop port.

Then he turned on the computer and watched the screen come to life.

The meeting was scheduled in five minutes, and Addan felt like he was preparing for a job interview.

"How do you think this is going to go?" Nicole asked.

Addan smiled. "I have a good feeling about it. I mean, she agreed to the meeting the morning after we prayed. That must be a sign, right?"

Nicole nodded but didn't seem convinced. "I hope so."

The laptop finished its startup process, and Addan went to his emails to find the link for the meeting.

Soon, he and Nicole were facing themselves on the screen and waiting for Damiyah to show up.

Thankfully, she wasn't late. Addan's heart leapt when he saw her face show up.

After a few moments of awkward silence, he said, "Hey, Damiyah, how are you and the kids?"

Damiyah wrinkled her nose. "We're fine. Just waiting on one other person."

"Huh?" Addan said, then the color drained from his face when another person popped up onto the screen: Damiyah's mother, Tamara.

"Hi, Tamara, what are you doing here?" Addan asked, trying to maintain an upbeat demeanor. Nicole fidgeted beside him.

Damiyah answered as Tamara gave a sly grin. "Don't be silly, Addan. You have your partner with you, so I have mine."

Addan wanted to protest but didn't want this conversation to go left before it began. He turned to his wife. "Nicole, is that okay with you?"

Nicole forced a smile. "Sure."

Damiyah's eyes narrowed. "It better be, and besides, her opinion doesn't matter anyway. She has no place with our children."

Addan didn't like the way Damiyah said, *our children,* especially with the comments she had been making to Mikayah, but he let it slide.

"Shall we get started?"

"We shall indeed," was Damiyah's snarky reply.

Addan's hopeful anticipation had become a tight knot in his stomach as the Zoom call interface displayed the connected parties. He launched into his plea with a shaky voice, "Damiyah, I really think we can come to an agreement that's fair for everyone, especially for the kids—"

But his words were like leaves caught in a whirlwind; Damiyah's expression was as unyielding as stone. "Fair? You call abandoning your family for her," she gestured disdainfully toward Nicole, "fair?"

Addan recoiled as if struck, the words stinging as they hit home. "We had issues long before Nicole came into the picture, Damiyah. You know that."

Nicole, her face a canvas of shock, interjected, "I never intended—"

Tamara's voice sliced through the tension, sharp and unwelcoming. "Oh, please! Save it. We all know your type."

The conversation spiraled rapidly, as Damiyah and Tamara launched into a vitriolic tirade against Nicole, their words laced with venom. The accusations hurled at Nicole were as personal as they were brutal, each one a dagger aimed straight at her heart.

Addan sat frozen; his voice lost as the women before him painted Nicole as the villain in a story he knew all too well was shaded with grey. Guilt and indecision paralyzed him, the lines of loyalty and truth blurring before his eyes.

Nicole, appearing blindsided by the attacks, looked to Addan for defense. "Are you going to just sit there and let them say these things to me?" Her voice was a mix of hurt and disbelief.

But when Addan failed to speak, failed to rise to her defense, the silence between them grew louder than the cacophony of insults being thrown. With a swift click, Nicole severed the connection, the screen going black like the sudden snuffing out of a candle.

The aftermath was a cold void. Nicole's swift departure left the kitchen feeling cavernous, her absence a gaping wound in the room's atmosphere. Addan sat there, the ghost of the conversation echoing in his ears, his inaction a chain around his neck.

He followed her out of the room. "Nicole... Nicole, wait!"

She whirled around, fire in her eyes. "What, Addan?"

He reached out to touch her, but she snatched away. "I'm sorry."

She crossed her arms. "Sorry for what? Because from where I'm standing, it looked like you agreed with everything they were saying about me."

Addan sputtered his next words. "No, I... Please, let me explain..."

"There's nothing to explain." Nicole's eyes clouded with hurt. "This whole time I was thinking we were a team, but now it's clear to me that you and Damiyah have unfinished business. Maybe I did break up your happy little arrangement."

Nicole's words were like a slap in the face, but Addan knew he deserved them.

When a comforter and pillow came tumbling down the stairs a few moments later, he knew what time it was.

He would give Nicole the night to cool off, then try again in the morning to apologize. Her assumptions couldn't be further from the truth. Addan was just as blindsided by Tamara and Damiyah's attacks as Nicole was.

Still, he should have snapped out of it sooner and defended her.

That night, as Addan's form lay contorted on the sofa, the comfort of their shared bed denied to him, the living room was a lonely island. And on this island, he was marooned by his own indecision, his silence a chasm between the life he wanted and the one he might have just lost.

Chapter 20

Nicole was stewing after her argument with Addan, and the fact that he didn't even attempt to come upstairs and apologize again rattled her.

Did he not care?

Maybe Damiyah's accusations were right. Maybe Addan was having second thoughts about being with her.

Nicole would not allow anyone to abuse her ever again. She had gone through too much turmoil with Breon to let Damiyah and her mother walk all over her.

The next morning, Nicole got up early to get ready for work because she didn't want to deal with Addan. When she emerged from the bedroom and walked downstairs, she mentally prepared herself to completely ignore him and walk out the door.

When she got to the bottom of the landing and saw the comforter and pillow neatly folded on top of the couch, her heart sank.

He left already? Nicole didn't hear him get up. She walked over to the window and peeked outside. Sure enough, Addan's car was gone.

Nicole felt numb.

Addan had gone to work and didn't bother to say anything to her.

Swallowing back her emotions, she exited the house, locking the door behind her and climbing into her car. She turned the key in the ignition and exited the driveway, resolving to focus on other things while she tried to figure out what to do about her rocky marriage.

When she got to work, she had barely been there an hour before a phone call came through from Briana's school.

"Hello?" Nicole answered immediately.

"Hello, Mrs. Roberts? This is Monica Lacey, Briana's principal. We have a situation at the school and need you to come immediately."

Nicole sat at attention. "Come immediately? What situation? What's going on with my daughter?"

A moment of silence passed, and then the principal said, "She's locked herself into the girl's bathroom and refuses to come out."

Nicole hightailed it to the school, her heart racing the entire way. Her mind scrambled with thoughts of her daughter as well as thoughts of Addan and Damiyah. Why was her world turning upside down like this?

After fighting through traffic, she made it to the school. Her heels clicked furiously against the floor as she approached the front desk and signed in, then was escorted to the third floor girl's bathroom. It was surrounded by a few teachers, a maintenance man, two members of the school's security team, and the principal.

"What's going on?" Nicole said as she approached the scene.

Monica faced her. "We don't know. We received a call from her teacher that she hadn't returned from the bathroom after twenty minutes. Someone came to check on her and found the door locked."

"Has she said anything? Is she okay in there?"

Monica nodded. "She seems to be okay. She's been talking to us, but she said the only person she will open the door for is her mother."

Nicole stepped closer to the door; her legs wobbly. "Briana? Honey, can you hear me?"

"Yes," was Briana's muffled reply.

"Can you come out of the bathroom please?"

A few moments passed before Briana said, "I didn't mean to cause trouble."

Something in her daughter's voice made the hairs on the back of Nicole's neck stand up. "You're not causing trouble, honey. Come on out. I'm right here."

Nicole waited with bated breath, and a few moments later, the lock clicked, and Briana opened the door.

She stared at the crowd formed around the bathroom, then rushed into her mother's arms, breaking down into a fit of sobs.

Nicole couldn't help but to well up too as she stared at the principal.

Monica's face was grim but understanding. "Come on, let's go speak with the school counselor."

Briana clung to Nicole as Monica led the way, and the security team took up the rear. When they made it to the counselor's office, Briana and Nicole sat next to each other.

Monica focused on Nicole. "I need to speak with you after you finish here."

Nicole nodded, and Monica closed the door behind her to ensure their privacy.

The counselor, Elizabeth, stared at Briana with concern. "Hey, Briana. Would you mind sharing with me what happened today?"

Briana looked at Nicole but didn't say anything.

Her daughter was afraid. Nicole approached the conversation delicately. "Elizabeth, everything we say in this room is confidential, right? Meaning that no one else will know what we talk about?"

Elizabeth nodded, seeming to catch on to what Nicole was trying to say. "Absolutely. As long as no crime has been committed, everything stays in this room."

Nicole faced her daughter. "Go ahead, baby. Tell her what happened." Nicole had a feeling it was about those girls.

Briana launched into her story, and Nicole's suspicions were confirmed. Kate and Ashley had been at it again, along with a few other girls.

Elizabeth listened and asked questions, every word spoken in a calm and compassionate manner. She didn't write a bunch of notes or use a clipboard like Nicole thought she would. The more Nicole listened, the more she wished she could open up to the woman herself.

After Briana shared everything that had been going on with her, Elizabeth faced Nicole, then Briana.

"Briana, would you be opposed to us holding a mediation meeting between yourself and the other girls?"

Briana's eyes widened. "What will happen in the meeting?"

Elizabeth held a hand up. "We won't discuss anything you don't want to. It will just be a discussion to see if we can't figure out what's going on here. We'll invite the other girls' parents too."

Once Briana heard that the other girls' parents would be involved in the meeting, she relaxed. "Okay, sure, that's fine," she said.

Elizabeth nodded, then waited a beat before making her next statement. "One other thing I'm thinking is that you and your mom might want to set up sessions with someone about everything you have been dealing with. It sounds like there might be other things going on besides what's happening with Kate and Ashley, am I right?"

Nicole's breath caught in her throat as Briana's face reddened. She nodded.

Elizabeth turned to Nicole. "I have a list of referrals to really good therapists in the area. I think we can help Nicole work through her issues, and of course, she can always come to me too."

By the time they left the office, Nicole was in a daze.

She almost forgot she had to meet with Monica, the principal. "Mrs. Roberts, I just wanted to let you know that we won't be holding this incident against Briana. We will have to make note of it, of course, but there won't be any suspensions or anything of that sort."

Nicole was grateful for that, but now her mind was on the fact that her daughter needed a therapist.

Chapter 21

Addan had crept out early to grab some coffees for him and Nicole in hopes they could talk about the argument that morning, but when he got back to the house, Nicole was already gone.

"Damn! I knew I should have called her." Addan looked down at his phone.

The line was long at the coffee shop's drive thru, and then he became stuck in traffic on his way back home. Now he had taken the morning off work for no reason.

Addan sat at the kitchen table staring into space for what felt like hours before he finally drank his coffee after reheating it. He put Nicole's in the refrigerator.

Sometime later, he was startled awake from his nap on the couch by a key turning at the front door. Addan rubbed his eyes then grabbed his cell phone, thinking he had overslept his alarm and had now missed a full day's work.

He hadn't.

Nicole entered the house followed by Briana.

Addan scrambled to his feet. "What are you doing home?"

Nicole stared at him with attitude. "What are you doing home? You were gone this morning when I got up."

"I took the morning off so we could talk. Then I went to get us coffee."

They stared at each other for a moment, then Nicole said, "If you took the morning off, that means you need to get ready for work now, right?"

As if answering her question, Addan's alarm blared. He silenced it. "I can take the rest of the day off." He stared at Briana, who stood nervously by the front door. "What's going on?"

Nicole shook her head. "Don't worry about it. You just go on to work." Then she added in a softer tone, "Briana and I need to talk."

Addan caught her drift. Something new must have happened at school.

He wordlessly climbed the stairs and took his shower, preparing for another day's work. When he exited the bathroom, Addan wondered if he should offer again to stay and help Nicole and Briana navigate the issue, then decided against it.

Bullying was a sensitive issue, and from the looks of it, Briana clung to her mother. He would never want to intrude upon that territory.

When he got home from work, Nicole was on the couch, and Briana was up in her bedroom.

"Hey," he said after slipping off his shoes, carrying his briefcase to his office and returning.

Nicole looked up at him. "Hey. Thanks for the coffee earlier."

Addan nodded. "Sorry for not calling you and telling you where I was."

She shrugged. "Don't mention it."

They stared at each other. Time to address the elephant in the room. "Nicole," Addan began, "Nothing Damiyah or her mother said was the truth. Damiyah and I did try to work things out at first, but once I put my best foot forward, she clammed up like she was no longer interested. I tried to woo her for months, but it got to the point where I felt like I was forcing it. It seemed like she had met someone else, so I gave up and started looking for someone myself. Then I met you."

Nicole nodded in understanding. "That's why she thinks I broke you guys up."

Addan tilted his head. "I guess so, but her logic is flawed if you ask me. If she wanted me back so bad, why act like she wasn't interested?"

Nicole shook her head. "Maybe she wanted you to chase her."

"Chase her?" Addan stared at Nicole incredulously. "We had already been married. What else did she want me to do?"

Nicole shrugged. "I don't know, Addan. Relationships are complicated."

"I hear that."

More silence fell between them, then Nicole asked a question that it seemed like she had been wrestling with. "Do you still have feelings for her?"

Addan's eyes widened. "For Damiyah? No, not really. I mean, I'll always have love for her as the mother of my kids, but with everything that's been happening lately, her actions have been a complete turn off."

Nicole seemed like she was with him until that last part. "Okay, but what if she hadn't started this custody battle? Did you have feelings for her before then?"

Addan understood what his wife was really asking. "Baby, I have no regrets about marrying you. Believe that. Damiyah and I had a good marriage at first, but things went south between us and stayed that way for years before we finally called it quits. We were able to be amicable after the divorce, but no, I have no desire to get back with her again."

"But you said you two tried to rekindle your relationship after the divorce, though," Nicole persisted.

"I mainly did that for the kids. It was obvious they wanted us back together, and I figured since me and Damiyah had been married before, maybe we could give it another try. But I can say without reservation it wasn't because I suddenly fell back in love with her. I figured those feelings might come back after a while, but they never did."

Silence fell between them once again until Nicole relaxed in her seat. "Good. That's what I needed to hear."

Addan turned to her with a playful expression. "Yeah? Don't tell me you were getting jealous, Mrs. Roberts. You know you hold the key to my heart."

"Really?" Nicole said, catching onto his game. "Why don't you come up to our bedroom and show me how much you love me then?"

"That I will do."

Chapter 22

It seemed like there was a night and day difference in Briana before and after her first session with her therapist.

After a few more sessions, Nicole was informed that her daughter had been dealing with undiagnosed social anxiety disorder.

When Briana's therapist shared the news, Nicole expected to have to comfort her daughter, but instead, it seemed as if a weight had been lifted from her shoulders.

"I knew it was something," Briana had said and cracked a smile.

Nicole was taken aback but happy until she learned that some of Briana's issues seemed to stem from her problems with Breon.

She listened in tears as her daughter shared with her that she had known about how her father abused her and had heard several of their arguments when they thought she wasn't listening.

"I kept feeling like I had done something to cause it," Briana said, her eyes pooling with tears.

"Absolutely not, baby," Nicole said. "Me and your father's issues have nothing to do with you."

Briana nodded. "I know that now, but sometimes I feel like if it wasn't for me, you would truly have a chance to be happy."

Those words took Nicole's breath away. Her throat constricted with pain. "No, baby. That couldn't be further from the truth. You are one of the few things on this earth that make me happy. I couldn't live without you."

Nicole and her daughter shared a long, heartfelt hug, and when they pulled away, it seemed Briana's fears had been calmed.

But Nicole's anxiety went through the roof.

Her issues with Breon were hurting her daughter. She couldn't allow this to go on without coming to some kind of resolution. The problem was that Breon was so difficult to deal with that she didn't know how to approach him.

Later that night, Nicole tossed and turned with yet another flashback.

After her first few botched attempts at relationships with men her age, Nicole tried a last-ditch effort and dated an older man, Alfred. He was in his late fifties, so Nicole figured there was no way Breon could penetrate the walls of their bond.

It turned out, Breon didn't have to, because Alfred had an ex of his own.

Nicole thought she and Alfred were in an exclusive relationship until one night she was at his house, and they were having a nice dinner. Suddenly, they heard a loud crash outside.

"Oh my God!" Nicole said, her heart racing at how loud the crash sounded. They opened the front door just as a crazed looking woman in a beat-up Honda reared back and crashed into Nicole's car. She had already slammed into the back of Alfred's car, and from the looks of it, it was totaled. Nicole turned to Alfred. "What the hell is going on?"

From the guilty look in Alfred's eyes, he had been cheating. "She's my ex," he explained, as the woman proceeded to crash into the neighbor's cars next. Thankfully the police arrived shortly after, and she was arrested, but Nicole's relationship with Alfred ended that night.

When Nicole woke up from her flashback, she gave therapy serious thought. It seemed to be working well for her daughter. Maybe she could give it a try. Maybe it would help her sort out her own anxieties and help her figure out how to deal with Breon effectively.

Chapter 23

Addan headed to the Chinese spot to pick up the food he and Nicole had ordered for the kids. Tonight was another attempt at family bonding. They were going to have a movie night where the kids picked a movie, then the adults, then they would go back and forth until everyone fell asleep.

Addan hoped this event would go better than the family picture.

After loading the huge bags into the car, Addan headed home. As the savory aromas of the food filled his nostrils, Addan grew excited about what the night would bring. The kids used to love movie nights when he and Damiyah did it. He hoped this would do the trick in resolving Mikayah's animosity toward his wife.

Unfortunately, as Addan approached the front door, he found that this wasn't the case.

Loud female voices could be heard from inside the house, and then a crash sounded.

"That's it!" Nicole's voice thundered. "You are getting out of my house tonight, little girl!"

"The hell I am!" Mikayah yelled back. "This house belongs to my mother and father. You can't make me go anywhere!"

"Sheesh!" Addan almost dropped his keys as he fumbled to get the door open. Once it opened, he saw the source of the crash. A huge wedding portrait of him and Nicole that had recently been delivered to their home, along with the hundred-dollar frame that surrounded it, was on the floor, the glass shattered in pieces everywhere.

Nicole's hair was all over the top of her head, and her face was red from yelling.

Mikayah didn't look much better, her fists clenched in defiance.

"Hey, what the hell is going on here?" Addan thundered.

Nicole turned to him with fire in her eyes. "Your daughter has disrespected me for the last time, Addan. I asked her a simple question, and she went on a rampage, throwing our wedding picture to the ground. I will not stand for this. No child will run me out of my own home."

Nicole stood flat footed and ready to fight.

From the looks of it, Mikayah wasn't ready to back down either.

Addan clicked his key fob. "Mikayah, get in the car."

His daughter whipped her head toward him, her eyes widened with surprise. "What?"

"I said get in the car now! And don't step on the glass or you might cut your feet."

Mikayah inched around the glass and walked toward Addan who was still holding the bags of food and drinks.

Addan handed her the car keys, and she went out toward the car. Addan wordlessly headed toward the kitchen and returned with the broom, sweeping up the glass from the floor. Nicole's eyes were now puffy and red as she shed tears of frustration. Briana looked lost, Addan Jr. seemed like he felt out of place, and Michael's features were etched with guilt. "Sorry, Daddy. Sorry, Nicole," he said and burst into tears.

"It's not your fault, son," Addan said, still upset about the glass.

Michael's voice trembled. "Yes, it is. If I wasn't trying so hard to hold the family together, Mikayah wouldn't be going crazy, and Nicole wouldn't have to cry. I ruined everything!" He burst into tears.

Within seconds, Addan dropped the broom and went to comfort his son. Michael's tears threw him for a loop because Michael was never the type to cry, even as a baby.

"Son, listen to me. None of this is your fault. Things are tough right now, but every family has its ups and downs. We're going to be just fine, understand? You didn't do this. No one did."

Michael seemed to take in his words, though it was clear he was still hurting.

"Go get in the car with your sister," Addan said and continued sweeping up the glass. Michael wordlessly grabbed his coat and exited the house.

Addan looked at Addan Jr. next, now worried that the issues with Michael and Mikayah would affect his oldest son too.

"You okay Champ?" he asked, testing the waters.

Addan Jr. nodded. "Can I go to my room and watch TV?"

Addan studied his son for signs that he wasn't okay like he said. After a few seconds, he relaxed. "Sure, go ahead."

Addan Jr. wasted no time hurrying up the stairs.

Addan finished cleaning the glass and walked over to his wife and Briana, who were still standing in place.

"Are you guys okay?"

They both nodded, and Nicole seemed to be calming down. "I'm sorry, Addan," Nicole said. "I didn't mean to yell at her, but she was being very disrespectful to me."

"I know. I'm gonna talk to them both, okay?"

"Are they going home?" Briana asked, still looking nervous. Her arms were wrapped around her belly.

"I'm not sure," Addan replied. "I'm going to see if I can get them to calm down and if we can try to turn this night around as a family. In the meantime, if you guys want to get started with a movie, go ahead. The food is right there." He gestured.

Addan gave Nicole a brief kiss, then exited the house.

When he climbed into the driver's seat of his car, he had no idea how the conversation was about to go or how to approach it, he just knew he needed to separate everyone so they could cool down.

Mikayah was crying in the front seat, while Michael looked lost in the back.

Addan put on some old school gospel tunes as he drove aimlessly through the streets. Once Mikayah's sniffles seemed to die down, he said, "You both know I will always love you, right?"

Neither child answered.

Addan turned the music down. "Kids, do you know that?"

"I guess so," Michael said from the back seat.

Addan glanced at him through the rearview. "I'm serious. I love you both, and I would never choose anyone over you or try to replace you. Ever. All I want is for us to be a family."

"But why does she have to be there?" Mikayah blurted. "Why can't you and Mommy get back together?"

Addan tensed, because Damiyah was the last person he wanted to discuss, but he tried his best to explain it.

"Mikayah, sometimes parents are better off friends than husband and wife. But that doesn't change the fact that we both love you guys with all our hearts. And Nicole loves you too. She doesn't want to replace your mom. She just wants to be your friend."

Silence filled the car as the kids seemed to take in Addan's words.

"You're not going to leave us? Ever?" Mikayah asked.

"No, baby. Never. As long as God gives me breath, I'm gonna be here."

After that, they seemed to calm, so Addan turned the music back up and headed home.

When they got there, awkward silence filled the living room until Addan suggested the kids pick a movie.

Michael chose a Marvel flick, and the girls agreed to watch it. Nicole fixed everyone plates of Chinese food and cups of soda, and Mikayah didn't refuse her food. Addan took that as a good sign, though he knew the work was far from over.

***

The next evening, when it was time for Damiyah to pick up the kids, Addan didn't let her skirt off like she usually did.

"Wait, I need to talk to you," he said, and he gave her a look that meant he was serious.

Damiyah rolled her eyes, then stepped outside of her car. "What do you want, Addan? I have things to do."

"I'm sure whatever things you have to do aren't more important than your kids."

She rolled her eyes again and cocked her head to the side with attitude.

"Can we step away from the car? I don't want them hearing our discussion."

Damiyah looked like she was about to protest at first, but she obliged. Once they were out of earshot, Addan launched into the story of what happened the previous day with Nicole and Mikayah.

"And?" She scoffed when he finished. "I hope you don't think I'm paying for your picture frame."

Addan gritted his teeth. "It's not about the picture frame, Damiyah! It's about the kids. Can't you see that whatever you're telling them about me at home is hurting them?"

Addan continued to explain and told her about how both Michael and Mikayah were afraid he was going to abandon them, and how Michael had broken down in tears and was stressing himself out trying to hold the family together.

Once Damiyah heard about that part of the story, her expression changed as if she suddenly realized what her actions were causing.

"Look, I'll talk to them, okay?" she said, but Addan knew that was as far as she would go with an apology.

"That's all I'm asking," he said. "But this time, please tell them the truth, Damiyah. I don't want our kids stressed out over something that's not happening."

Chapter 24

Although there weren't any more blowups over the weekend between Nicole and Mikayah, Nicole still felt horrible about how she had screamed at Addan's daughter.

The girl had disrespected her, true enough, but Nicole couldn't deny that some of her frustration had nothing to do with Mikayah and had more to do with everything else that was going on.

Breon had been calling her phone over the past couple of days, but Nicole hadn't answered. She didn't want to deal with any drama from him and that was all he brought to her door.

Sooner or later, she knew she would have to talk to him, but Nicole would rather the conversation happen later. She still wasn't over the last stunt he pulled, getting her all riled up about Briana signing up for a tattoo, only to find out no such appointment had been made, and he staged the whole argument just to start trouble.

Nicole got through her whole workday without any issues, then as soon as she pulled down the street to get home, Breon called again.

Nicole sighed. "Whatever. Might as well get it over with." She pressed the Answer button on her dashboard.

"Hello?"

Breon's thunderous voice filled her car. "Nicole, what the hell is wrong with you?"

Nicole sighed. "What do you mean, what's wrong with me, Breon?"

"What's this I'm hearing about Briana going to see a counselor? And why didn't you tell me my daughter was being bullied?"

Nicole fell silent. She should have told Breon what was going on, but she didn't feel like getting into it with him now. "Look, I'll call you later," she said, but Breon cut her off.

"No, you'll talk to me now! How dare you hold something back from me like this? That girl is my daughter too, not just yours. What if something had happened to her, huh, Nicole? This is why I could never deal with you. You are such a stupid woman. Never know how to handle business when it's time to. All you do is..."

Nicole remained silent as Breon rained verbal blows at her from his end of the line, holding back no insult as he unleashed his fury in her direction.

Her eyes filled with tears at the vile remarks he made about her character and capacity to raise their daughter, then when he was about to go into her looks, the line suddenly went silent.

Nicole's eyes widened at first. She thought he had hung up, but then she turned and noticed that Addan had pulled up next to her, and his car must have picked up her Bluetooth signal.

Breon's muffled voice could be heard in Addan's car.

Nicole had half a mind to press the button on her dashboard to hang up on her ex, but another part of her was tired of running from this conversation. If Addan was ever going to get a glimpse of the type of treatment she endured from Breon, he was getting it now.

Nicole stared as Addan listened in silence for a few moments, then he signaled for her to hang up the phone.

She obeyed.

He stepped out of his car, and she did the same, walking around to face him. Nicole was nervous because she couldn't read Addan's expression.

"Was that your ex? Breon?"

She nodded.

He swallowed. "Is that how he always talks to you?"

Nicole's eyes filled with tears, and she nodded again.

Addan's next words were cool, calm, and collected. "When is the next time he picks up Briana?"

Nicole was puzzled by this question, but she told him. "He's supposed to get her this weekend."

"Cool." Addan gave her an eerie smile. "I'll bring her to the drop off location."

Something about Addan's smile made Nicole nervous. Now she wished she hadn't let him get an earful of Breon's abusive tirade. Nicole wanted to protest, but Addan seemed firm in his decision. Her heart told her to let her husband handle it.

Chapter 25

Addan and Briana engaged in light chatter as he drove Nicole's car to the meetup location to let Breon take his daughter.

Nicole had mentioned in the past that Breon had abused her when they were together and that he still liked to harass her now with petty arguments, but Addan had no idea the man felt so comfortable talking to his wife in the way he had unintentionally heard the other day. His first thought was to pay a visit to Breon's neighborhood and introduce him to his friends, Smith & Wesson, but Addan was a changed man.

He would handle this the adult way first, and if Breon wasn't receptive to that, then he would resort to other means.

When they arrived at the location, Breon's car was already there.

He jumped out and stalked over like he was ready to start another fight, but he stopped short when he saw Addan step out of the vehicle instead of Nicole.

Breon's eyes widened. "Hey, man. What are you doing here?"

Addan studied Breon and immediately knew what type of man he was. He took a step forward, and Breon fidgeted.

"I heard the conversation you had with my wife the other day. Your call came through on my Bluetooth."

Breon looked like he had seen a ghost. Addan turned to Briana. "Hey, Briana. Why don't you go wait in your daddy's car?"

Breon quickly gave his daughter his keys, then when she ran off to go sit in the car, he gave Addan an uneasy glance like he wasn't sure how to take him.

Addan dropped his cordial smile and gave Breon a menacing glare. "I'm only going to tell you this one time, brother to brother." He gestured between himself and Nicole's ex as he spoke. "You don't call or text my wife ever again. If you have something to say to her you contact me. Understood? And just so you know, I will be dropping Briana off to you from now on. I see no reason for you and Nicole to have any further interactions. I think that's the best way to handle things going forward, don't you?"

Addan stared at Breon without blinking, daring him to defy his suggestion.

Breon stared for a few moments then relented. "Alright, man. No doubt."

Addan relaxed. "Cool. I knew you'd see it my way. Take down my number and erase Nicole's."

Breon took Addan's number. At first, Addan was going to stand there and watch him erase Nicole's number but decided against it. He didn't want to emasculate the man, just to send him a message.

"Y'all have a good weekend. I'll be back tomorrow to pick her up."

"No doubt," Breon said, and went back to his car.

Nicole was full of questions when Addan got home, but Addan didn't give her any details about the conversation.

"Just know that it's handled, babe," he said. "Breon won't be bothering you anymore."

Chapter 26

Nicole waited a whole month for the other shoe to drop and for Breon to rear his ugly head again, but he didn't. She didn't know what Addan had said to the man, but whatever it was had worked.

It was over.

Once she realized the years of trials and torment had ceased, Nicole felt like a huge weight had been lifted off her. Like she could finally be free.

No more looking over her shoulder and waiting for Breon to file a new court case. No more insults. No more manipulation. She was no longer under Breon's psychological control.

"Babe, you okay?"

Nicole looked up to see Addan standing in their bedroom doorway, watching her intently.

She shrugged. "Yes, I'm fine."

"You don't look fine. What's going on?"

She welled up. "I'm just thinking about how it's finally over between me and Breon. He hasn't contacted me in over a month."

Addan came over and sat on the bed next to her. "I told you it was handled. I wouldn't have expected him to reach out to you again after our conversation."

She turned to her husband. "What did you say to him?"

Addan smiled. "Don't worry about that. I just stepped into my role as your husband. That's my job, to protect you."

Nicole grew hot suddenly. "Protect me, huh? You did your job?"

Addan licked his lips. "Indeed, I did."

The more Nicole stared at Addan, the more she couldn't believe how blessed she was. She had never had a man protect her before.

Then the weight of that revelation became too much, and she broke down in tears.

Addan's arms immediately encircled her. "Baby, what's wrong?"

"Addan, you don't understand." Nicole let loose. She let it all out, from the beginning, and told him the whole story of everything Breon had done to her and about all the flashbacks she had been having lately, and how it all culminated in him finally leaving her alone for good.

Addan sat and listened, holding her the entire time.

Nicole felt like she had talked for hours by the time she finished, but another burden had been lifted from her heart.

"Babe, after everything you told me, I think we need to sign you up for therapy. You can't hold that all inside you. It's a wonder you haven't broken down yet."

Nicole nodded, thankful that her husband understood her situation.

That night, Addan ran Nicole a hot bubble bath and lit some candles, putting on slow music to help her ease her mind.

After that, he gave her a full body massage, and that was when the real fireworks started.

***

Nicole took heed to her husband's advice. She sought out a therapist to help her deal with her issues. After one session with Bridgette, she realized she should have done this a long time ago.

It turned out that Breon wasn't the only issue she dealt with. There were a lot of thoughts, feelings, emotions, and experiences she had pent up over time.

"Hmm, maybe all those thoughts I had about a ticking time bomb were about me," she confessed.

Bridgette nodded. "I'm glad you came to the right place, Nicole. We're going to get through this, step by step."

After another month, Nicole felt lighter. It was scary because for the first time in her life, she felt like there was nothing wrong with her.

That caused her to break down again.

"Why was I finding it normal to feel like something had to be wrong with me? Why is feeling alright a problem? Am I that jacked up, Bridgette?"

As usual, Bridgette never judged. She only offered a listening ear and steered Nicole toward various tools to help her on her healing journey.

Nicole used two journals: a Bible journal that helped her see herself from God's standpoint, and a regular journal where she wrote down every memory she had been holding onto since childhood. As she watched the pages of both journals fill up, Nicole felt like she had some bestsellers on her hands.

"Bridgette, I can't believe how my life is changing," Nicole said after another couple of months. "It's like I feel so empowered. Like I can take on the world."

Ever the anchor, Bridgette encouraged her but also kept her grounded. "That's wonderful, Nicole. Remember, good and bad things happen to good and bad people. It's how we manage the things that happen to us that determine the outcomes."

It was as if God had handpicked Bridgette for Nicole. Every time she had a question, confession, or revelation, Bridgette always seemed to have the right words to say.

Even when she didn't say anything, her silence helped Nicole process her thoughts too.

Her life wasn't perfect, and probably never would be, but it was getting tremendously better.

Chapter 27

It was the weekend, and as usual, Addan had the kids. Summer was approaching soon, and Addan wondered what things would be like once he had them full time again.

He was still getting used to the whiplash of having them stripped from him, and now he had to turn around and get used to them being with him for the summer, only to be stripped away again when fall came around.

"How do people do this?" he mused.

This type of custody arrangement was like a foreign land that Addan was unsuccessfully navigating.

He had told Nicole to seek counseling when she broke down and told him about all her issues, but now Addan wondered if he might need to see somebody.

The ironic thing was that Addan had a degree in psychology and had served several years as a therapist before moving on to business consulting. He should have recognized the signs in himself immediately, but he had been so busy putting fires out that he hadn't considered it.

Then he thought of Damiyah.

If he were honest with himself, Addan held hatred in his heart for that woman. It was something he couldn't fully grasp because at one time, he had been head over heels in love with her, but once she took his children from him, it was like she snatched away a piece of his soul.

Addan snapped out of his thoughts and considered what he just realized. "Wow, I do need a counselor."

He knew the right steps to take but wasn't sure how to go about it.

Then he thought of the kids and felt guilty. The whole time since the divorce, the kids had been suffering. Mikayah had been lashing out, and Michael internalized it to the point where if he hadn't broken down that day in tears, Addan never would have realized the burden his son was trying to carry.

They all needed help.

"What's the matter with me?" Addan said to his reflection in the bathroom mirror, wondering how he had dropped the ball on something so important.

Then he gave himself some grace. That was something he always told his clients when he served as a therapist. Sometimes from the outside looking in, answers seemed obvious, and the steps to approach healing seemed easy, but that was until you were in the situation.

Sometimes in the midst of the fire, you were so busy trying to put it out that you missed the flames.

It was a lot to think about, but Addan knew action needed to be taken soon.

***

When Addan went downstairs to rejoin his family, the kids were sitting silently on their cell phones. The silence became deafening in Addan's ears.

"Mikayah, Michael, can I talk to you two for a moment?" The kids looked up at him as if they were afraid.

Addan didn't like this. He never wanted to put that kind of fear in their hearts.

He gestured toward the kitchen. Briana and Addan Jr. looked up from their phones as well but didn't say anything.

When they made it to the kitchen, Addan began the conversation. "How are you two feeling?"

He studied Mikayah, then Michael.

"About what?" Mikayah asked, looking guilty.

"About everything. Me, your mom, our divorce, everything."

Her eyes filled up. "Daddy, I know you said everything would work out, but it doesn't seem to be working. Why can't you and Mommy just get back together? Nicole is nice and everything, but I feel like we were all happy when you and Mommy were in the same home."

Those words broke Addan's heart, but it also confirmed that his family indeed needed counseling.

Michael shared the same sentiments as his sister, and Addan tried his best to alleviate their broken hearts, but he knew he couldn't do all the work by himself.

They would need reinforcements.

Chapter 28

Addan was working late tonight, so Briana and Nicole had a few hours to themselves. "I got my report card today," Briana said with a smile, and the way she announced it let Nicole know it was about to be good news.

Briana handed her the envelope, and Nicole scanned it, her eyes widening as she saw all the A's going down the line.

"You got all A's!" She stared at her daughter in amazement.

Briana beamed. "Yup."

Briana had always been a smart girl, and she never earned bad grades, but for her to earn straight A's for the first time showed that something had changed in her life.

"I'm so proud of you, baby," Nicole said, tears in her eyes.

"I'm proud of you too," Briana said to her surprise.

"What are you proud of me for?" Nicole asked.

Briana shrugged. "I feel like you are finally seeing yourself."

Nicole fell silent at those words. Her first thought was to feel like scum, because she understood the implications of Briana's statements. She hadn't realized how deeply the years of trauma and abuse had become embedded in her psyche and seeped out into her everyday life and perceptions, but after several months of therapy with Bridgette, Nicole was learning to recognize issues as they rose to the surface, process them, and then let them go. She was going to continue to move forward. The Bible said she was a new creature and that old things had passed away. She was precious in God's eyesight, and He was helping through her healing journey as well.

Nicole turned to her daughter. "Thank you, baby. I needed that." They shared a hug, then Nicole stood from the couch. "Come on. Let's go."

Briana wrinkled her nose. "Where are we going?"

"Let's get some ice cream or cake or something! Girl, we got to celebrate those straight A's!"

Briana giggled, and they headed to the car.

They arrived at the ice cream spot, and as they were approaching the line, Briana stopped short.

"What?" Nicole said, looking back at her daughter and wondering if she forgot her phone in the car.

Then Nicole followed Briana's gaze and saw Ashley and Kate, the two girls who had bullied her daughter, standing in line with their mothers.

Nicole looked back at Briana. "Do you want to go somewhere else?"

Briana stared at the girls for a few moments longer before shaking her head. "No. Here is fine."

Nicole's heart swelled with pride as her daughter led the way into the ice cream parlor. Ashley and Kate turned around and noticed her, but they didn't say anything. They nodded in greeting, then continued their chat.

Nicole watched as Briana held her head high while they waited their turn to place their orders.

When they left the store, Briana exhaled in the parking lot, her limbs shaking, and her body jittery.

"I can't believe I did that!" she gushed, staring at Nicole in amazement.

Nicole beamed, not quite sure where her daughter was going with her excitement.

"Baby steps," Briana proclaimed, and Nicole understood. "My therapist said we have to take baby steps."

Chapter 29

Nicole woke up the following morning to several back-to-back pings on her cell phone. She groggily turned over to silence the incessant sounds, and then she realized it was someone messaging her on social media.

"Who is that?" Addan murmured, awakened from the sound too.

Nicole's first thought was that Breon had come back to do more damage, but to her surprise, it wasn't him.

"It's Damiyah!" she said, sitting up on her side of the bed, fully alert as she swiped her screen and put in her passcode to read the messages.

"Damiyah?" Addan repeated, then sat up in bed too. "What's she saying?"

Nicole looked at her husband in shock. "She's apologizing."

Nicole angled her phone screen so she and Addan could read the messages as they came in together.

Nicole, I owe you an apology.

You and I got off on the wrong foot and it was mostly my fault.

Woman to woman, I'm sorry for how I treated you and how it's caused a rift between you and my daughter.

I guess I just became afraid that my kids would start gravitating toward you since you were now living with their father.

I know what I did was wrong, and I own it. I'm sorry.

"Wow," Addan said, looking at Nicole in amazement. "This is... big of her."

"Big indeed."

Nicole wasn't sure how to respond. She accepted Damiyah's apology, but she would prefer that all the drama ceased.

As if Damiyah had heard the thoughts and translated them into text messages, more pings sounded.

Nicole swiped her screen again, and she and Addan continued to read.

Going forward, I would like for us to figure out the right way to coparent.

I know it can't be good for the kids to see their parents hold animosity toward one another.

If you are open to it, I would like us to have a conversation.

I promise to do my part going forward for the betterment of the kids.

"Now she's talkin'," Addan commented, and Nicole smiled.

After it seemed Damiyah had ceased, Nicole wrote back.

Damiyah, I accept your apology, and I agree. We need to do what's right for the kids.

Let's set up that meeting and commit to do better moving forward.

Chapter 30

Addan was blown away not only by the fact that Nicole and Damiyah had a cordial conversation a few days later, but also at the fact that Damiyah brought up the idea of family counseling.

"Am I in a parallel universe?" he joked when he heard the good news.

It seemed that the storm was over and that it was time to pick up the pieces and forge a genuine bond as a family.

Addan didn't want to get too excited at the possibilities because he knew things could still go left from here, but he allowed himself hope at the least.

When the weekend rolled around, Addan and Nicole sat the kids down and talked to them about the idea of family counseling to help them transition to their new reality.

The kids seemed to be on board with the idea, even Mikayah, and for that, Addan was grateful.

Now it was time to put in the work.

Once the kids agreed to the idea of counseling, Addan went to work searching for the best counselors in the area. He narrowed his list down to three, then created a group text between himself, Nicole, and Damiyah.

Here are the professionals I found in our area, he wrote. *How about you ladies check them out and let me know which one you want to go with.*

Within seconds, Damiyah responded. *I already set us up an appointment with a counselor. We're supposed to meet next week.*

Addan's eyes widened at this news.

Damiyah had already set up an appointment? Why hadn't she mentioned anything? Addan's first thought was that she was back to her old schemes. He wouldn't put it past Damiyah to hire one of her friends as their counselor so the woman could bash him and Nicole the entire session, driving a further wedge between him and the children.

He was about to write to her and say he would prefer someone neutral when Nicole chimed into the chat.

That's great, Damiyah. Send us the details, and we'll be there.

Once Addan saw those words, he was pissed. Why hadn't Nicole reached out to him first before agreeing to see Damiyah's counselor? Couldn't she see this was a trick? Damiyah couldn't be trusted, and Addan was about to remind his wife of that reality when she called him.

"Hey," she said when he answered. "I hope you didn't get upset at the fact that I agreed to see Damiyah's counselor. I just felt in my spirit we should give it a try since she went out of her way to choose someone and set up an appointment for us."

Addan fell silent for a moment. "Yeah, Nicole, I get that, but what if it's a trick? What if this so-called counselor is one of her friends? What if they start another argument like what happened on the Zoom call with her and her mother?"

Nicole waited a beat before responding. "I understand why you would think that way given our history, but isn't part of building a relationship giving the other person a chance? What if she's sincere, Addan?"

He couldn't deny his wife had a point, even if he didn't like it.

Addan reluctantly agreed to move forward.

Chapter 31

After Nicole hung up the phone with Addan, a sense of conviction filled her heart. She had just essentially forced her husband to work with Damiyah's plan, yet she still held great resentment in her heart against Breon.

It was for good reason, especially after all he put her through, but Bridgette had mentioned during their last session that eventually she would have to find a way to forgive him as part of her healing process.

Nicole was taken aback by that proclamation because she wanted no parts of that man ever again, but Bridgette's explanation made her think.

"It doesn't mean you have to rebuild a relationship with Breon, or even have a conversation with him, for that matter. This is more about your healing and peace of mind. You went through a lot because of your relationship with him. You can't heal from the effects without healing from the source."

Those words had struck Nicole in a way she wasn't comfortable with.

She hadn't shared this with Bridgette, but the woman had probably gleaned how she was feeling based on her lack of response.

After those words were spoken, Nicole cut the session short and left.

How could Bridgette suggest forgiving Breon? Had she not heard about the thirty-plus court cases, the financial strain and homelessness, the physical, psychological, and emotional abuse, the slander and accusations, and the years of torment and manipulation? And she had to forgive him?

"Hell no!" Were her first words, then conviction filled her heart, and she knew God was telling her to do the same.

Nicole told herself this might be where she got off the train.

The healing journey had been great when she was learning about herself and about how God saw her and about her good qualities she had overlooked while focusing on the bad.

But now God wanted her to extend this newfound grace to that monster?

She couldn't deal.

Then Briana's face flashed through her mind, and Nicole became convicted all over again.

Briana had shared previously that part of her anxiety came from Nicole and Breon's issues. If Nicole never forgave Breon, was there a chance it would negatively impact her daughter?

She didn't want to take that chance, but at the same time, she was at a crossroads.

Nicole swiped the fresh tears that had rolled down her cheeks as she wrestled with those heavy thoughts.

Then she let out an angry prayer she wasn't sure the Lord would even hear. "If you want me to forgive that man, you're gonna have to show me how!"

Chapter 32

Summertime rolled around, and the family had to adjust to yet another shift in their reality. Now Addan was thrust back into the responsibility of having the kids full time, and Nicole had to get used to it too.

Things still weren't a hundred percent perfect between herself and Mikayah, but Nicole had resolved that she wasn't going to try to force herself on Addan's daughter. She would show Mikayah that she was a good person, and hopefully, the girl would come to her.

Addan was over the moon with excitement despite his nervousness about how the summer would go. "You kids ready for Disney?" he asked, glee filling his features.

The kids were thrown for a loop for a second, because Addan and Nicole hadn't uttered a word about the two-week vacation they were planning to kick off the summer.

When Addan's announcement trickled through their ears, Michael was the first one to break out into a happy dance.

Mikayah did the same, and Briana and Addan Jr. looked excited too.

Nicole was happy Mikayah didn't immediately ask if she would be forced to sit next to her on the plane or something. This was a good sign.

They boarded their flight the next day, and soon, they were swept up in the world of Disney. Nicole couldn't deny that she was having just as much fun as the kids, though there was a lot of walking involved in the huge park.

The food was delicious, though and the entertainment was nonstop, so if the kids were happy, so was she.

At the end of the night, the kids went into their adjoining suite to fall asleep, while Addan and Nicole took their showers in the parent's suite. The hotel they were staying in was connected to the park, so it would make for easy access traveling back and forth.

Nicole and Addan sat on their balcony enjoying the view and sipping on a glass of wine after a long day of excitement and joy.

"Did you see the look on Michael's face when he got off that last ride?" Addan asked with a chuckle.

Nicole giggled as well. "Yes, it was priceless. I'm so glad we grabbed a picture of it. The kids are going to have so many memories to look back on from this trip alone."

Addan nodded. "This was a great idea."

Nicole yawned. "Great idea indeed."

He gave her a look of mock-concern. "Don't tell me you're getting tired, Mrs. Roberts. The night is still young, and I'm up for some more excitement."

Nicole grew hot at her husband's not-so-subtle suggestion. "Excitement, huh? What do you have in mind?"

"I can show you better than I can tell you."

***

The rest of the Disney trip went well, and when it was time to leave, the kids were sad to go. That was a great sign. Nicole was ready to get back home, but she was open to coming back to the park again.

They arrived home on a Friday, took Saturday to recuperate, then headed to church on Sunday morning.

Nicole enjoyed the worship experience with Addan and the kids. It was something she felt like she could get used to now that everyone was getting along.

Unfortunately, the good days came to a screeching halt when Nicole and Addan were awakened in the middle of the night to Briana's frantic knocks on their bedroom door.

"Mom! Mommy! Daddy's gonna hurt himself!"

Nicole's eyes popped open at the sound of her daughter's desperate pleas. She shot out of bed and rushed over to open the door.

Addan sat up too, wiping his eyes.

"What are you talking about, honey?" Nicole said, then when Briana thrust her cell phone in Nicole's face, Nicole saw what she meant.

Breon was Live on his profile drinking and smoking and talking about ending his life. As Nicole listened for a few moments, she gleaned that he was upset because his fiancée recently left him, and he just learned his father had passed.

"I just don't feel like I have nothing to live for, y'all," he was saying, and Nicole almost sucked her teeth at the number of women who were commenting and begging him to change his mind.

"My life is over. My daddy is gone, my woman left me, and I lost my job of fifteen years. It's over."

Briana was hysterical, and Nicole had half a mind to call Breon and curse him out for carrying on like this. Didn't he know there was a chance his daughter would see what he was saying?

"Mommy, we have to help him!" Briana was beside herself with grief, tears streaming down her face at her father's antics.

Part of Nicole felt heartless for not feeling compassion for Breon, then a tiny part of her felt bad for him. Though Breon's father was not the best of men, Breon did love him, and they were very close.

Nicole looked at Addan.

His expression was serious. "What do you want to do?"

Nicole did not want to deal with this in the middle of the night, but she could not in good conscience let it go. If Breon was serious and ended his life, Nicole would never forgive herself.

"Let's try to call him," she offered.

"No, Mommy, we need to go over there!" Briana wailed.

Addan was already on the phone as Breon's Live video ended. "Hey, man, just wanted to check in with you. Briana showed us your video. You alright?"

Addan listened for a few moments and then his expression changed.

At that moment, fear gripped Nicole's heart as she realized Breon's video wasn't just another manipulative ploy for attention. The man was seriously considering harming himself.

"Okay, I hear you," Addan was saying. "How about you don't make any decisions right now. What if we can get you someone to talk to? Would you be open to that? Your daughter loves you, man."

Addan listened for a few more moments, then he said, "Okay, man, we're on our way."

He hung up the phone, and Briana called her father. Thankfully, he answered. "Daddy? Daddy, don't do anything!" she exclaimed, hiccupping as she tried to calm herself down. "We're coming, okay?"

Addan and Nicole stared at each other.

"Addan, we can't bring all the kids out there," Nicole said.

"I know," he agreed. "I'll bring Briana, and we'll get him some help. You stay here with Addan Jr., Michael and Mikayah."

Nicole was reluctant to let her daughter go out there not knowing what condition Breon would be in when they arrived, but she reluctantly nodded. "Okay. Keep my daughter safe, Addan."

"You already know." They shared a kiss, then left, Briana still talking to her father as they walked out the door.

After they left, Nicole found herself checking her phone every few minutes and steadily praying for Breon in between.

She couldn't believe she found herself praying for a man who caused her so much pain, but at the same time, she didn't want anything to happen to him.

***

Thankfully, Addan and Briana were able to convince Breon to get himself checked into the crisis unit at the Emergency Room. Briana wanted to stay the night with him, but Addan promised her they would come back in the morning.

Briana stayed up all night, which meant Nicole couldn't sleep either.

The next morning, Addan took Briana back to the hospital, and Breon seemed to be in better spirits.

Nicole thanked God for that, and she felt a piece of her anger at the man chip away.

Chapter 33

Today was Mikayah's birthday, and Addan was throwing her a birthday/eighth grade graduation celebration. All the family on both sides were invited, which meant Damiyah and her mother would be there as well.

Addan was incredibly proud of his daughter, and he was hoping that everyone's joy over Mikayah's accomplishments would overshadow any lingering resentments that may be held between the adults in the family.

Their family counseling sessions had been going relatively well, which Addan took as a good sign. So far there hadn't been any huge blowouts. A few sarcastic comments were made on both sides, mostly from him and Damiyah, and Addan felt bad that he and his ex-wife seemed to be the main contributors to the family's problems.

One day they would get it together, but it would take time.

As everyone began to arrive, smiling and bearing gifts, Addan had a good feeling. Damiyah and her mother came together, and they both carried huge gift bags with them too. Addan expected nothing less, but the real test would be in how they approached him. When Damiyah and her mother both gave cordial greetings to him and Nicole, Addan relaxed.

Today would be focused on Mikayah after all.

***

Nicole was enjoying the party, though she was initially nervous when Damiyah and Tamara entered the hall.

Thankfully, neither of them said a cross word to her, and Damiyah even complimented her hairstyle.

"Thank you!" Nicole beamed.

"I love that dress, Tamara, and you are working those heels, Damiyah."

After the pleasant greeting, the women walked away, but Nicole caught Mikayah staring at their interaction out of the corner of her eye.

Nicole turned in Mikayah's direction, but the girl quickly looked away and began chatting with one of her cousins.

The DJ played a good selection of songs, and soon the party was officially underway. They played games, had a soul train line, did the Cha Cha Slide, and overall had a great time.

When the party was nearing its end, Nicole caught Damiyah whispering in the DJ's ear.

"Alright now, y'all! We're going to have one last event before we close. The birthday girl slash graduate is going to open her gifts!"

Nicole's heart dropped when she heard the news because this could go really left. She looked at Addan and was about to tell him that maybe he should redirect the DJ, but he seemed to be happy about the idea.

Nicole waited with bated breath as everyone surrounded the gift table.

Mikayah sat on a pink princess throne and ripped open the boxes, pulling gifts out of the bags.

Nicole watched as Mikayah grew more excited with each gift, from a brand-new bicycle, to money, to gift cards to clothing stores, and the like.

Her heart pounded as Mikayah drew closer to her gift. Nicole hoped she liked it. It wasn't much—just a makeup kit all the girls Mikayah's age seemed to be raving about, but Nicole hoped her gift would go over well.

When Mikayah got to Nicole's gift, it seemed as if she took her time unwrapping the paper.

When she pulled out the brand-new makeup kit, including a mirror, everyone oohed and ahhed. "Wow, thanks Nicole!" she said, smiling from ear to ear.

Nicole's heart leapt, and then she was taken aback when Mikayah shot out of her throne to give her a brief hug.

The hug lasted half a second, but Nicole became so overcome with emotion that she had to excuse herself to the bathroom.

Mikayah had never hugged her before.

Chapter 34

It seemed like Summer had flown by, and now it was time for fall.

Also time for the kids to go back to living with their mothers full time. Although Addan wrestled with the idea of giving them up at the end of the summer, he had to find a way to come to grips with the fact that things had changed and the life he was used to with his children wasn't there anymore.

Now he had to pave a new path and maintain their connection in a different way. Seeing them only on weekends was a grievous blow, but Addan couldn't deny that it freed up his time to focus on hobbies. He had completed several DIY projects around the house in his spare time.

Part of him was still bitter and felt like he could still have done his DIY projects with the kids there and even had them help him, but he fought it back down.

He had to decide: was he going to live the rest of his life in bitterness or was he going to move forward and make the best of the new arrangement?

The obvious answer was clear, but Addan had to force himself to let go.

Part of what helped him to do this was realizing that the kids were starting to adjust to the new arrangement now that the family counseling sessions had been going on for a few months.

They seemed to be in much better spirits, and Mikayah had even made a comment the other day about being excited to start at her new high school.

When Addan thought of high school, his mind immediately shot to college. What was he going to do then? The kids would inevitably grow up, branch out, and start their own lives as adults.

If he maintained his bitter attitude toward Damiyah the whole time they were teens, he could miss out on valuable memories and time well spent. Life was too short and unpredictable to hold onto the pain.

Addan let it go.

When Michael and Mikayah went back with their mother, they shared a tearful goodbye with Addan and Nicole, though they all knew they would be seeing each other again on the weekend.

"Alright now, y'all are making me jealous!" Damiyah joked, and they all shared a laugh.

Addan lightened up.

As long as his kids were safe and happy, he had no choice but to feel the same.

"We made it through the summer!" Nicole said when they closed the door and Briana went up to her room to play on her phone.

Addan Jr. had already been picked up by his mother earlier in the day. Thankfully, Addan Jr. seemed to be faring well despite all the turmoil the family had gone through. Addan believed it was probably because his relationship with Niya, Addan Jr.'s mother, was amicable since their divorce.

Addan sighed. "Indeed, we did."

"Wanna watch some movies with me?" Nicole said with a mischievous smile, causing Addan's heart to skip a beat. "It's been a while since we did a little Netflix and chill."

"Netflix and chill, huh?" he said. "Sounds like a plan."

Chapter 35

It was hard to believe, but an entire year had passed, and today was Addan and Nicole's first anniversary.

The day went well, with the kids throwing them a party to celebrate.

Addan and Nicole were surprised at the gesture, but they pulled it off nicely, with each of them giving a short heartfelt speech at the end of the night about what Addan and Nicole's union meant to them.

At the end of the night, Addan and Nicole sat in their bedroom drinking a bottle of champagne and reflecting on all they had gone through.

"I think the hardest part of this year for me was seeing you go through what you went through with your kids," Nicole said, taking a sip from her flute.

Addan nodded. "It was tough, but you were my rock, all while you were going through struggles of your own."

Nicole nodded.

Thankfully, Breon had pulled out of his depression and seemed to be doing better. He got back with his fiancée, and he and Briana talked all the time.

Briana was doing much better as well. She had mustered up the courage to go to her school's dance at the end of the year and stayed the whole night. When she came home, she and Nicole had gushed about it and some boy had asked for her number. Nicole was nervous about that because she wasn't sure how she felt about her daughter dating, but Addan took notes, because Mikayah was right behind her. She was entering high school now, and boys would likely go to the forefront of her mind too.

Michael seemed to be adjusting well entering his final year of middle school. He was a bright kid who loved robotics and anime and was always the life of the party wherever he went. Addan didn't know where the kid got his energy because neither he nor Damiyah were as outgoing as their son.

Michael was growing into his own man, and Addan couldn't be prouder.

Thankfully, Damiyah and Addan's relationship had gotten much better, and Addan felt most of the bitterness leave his heart.

He would always be a work in progress, but he was happy about how far he had come.

"What do you think the next year will bring?" Nicole asked, and Addan chuckled because he knew they both hoped that next year was nothing like the one they just experienced.

"I'll say it like this," he said. "With all we endured in the last year, I feel like we can get through anything together. You're the right woman for me, and I see it more every day. But..." He stared into his wife's eyes. "If next year was full of nothing but peace, I would have no objections."

Nicole wholeheartedly agreed, clinking her flute against her husband's. "Let's toast to that. To us."

Addan smiled, then leaned in close for a kiss. "To us."

The End

About the Authors

Coach Darrell Dr. White was born and raised in Baltimore, Maryland. His passion for helping people to become the best version of themselves began when he embarked upon a career in personal/group fitness training in 2003. He often tells an amazing transformation story about a client that he trained for several months. Three months after transitioning into training independently, the client regained all of the weight previously lost. When Darrell inquired about how the client regained the weight, the client mentioned that it was due to stress-eating as a result of a failing relationship. Darrell immediately recognized that he had to do much more to help his clients because what we see externally can be a direct result of what's occurring internally. He had to pursue a more holistic approach to training clients, but he didn't know how.

In 2010, Darrell earned a dual Bachelor of Arts degree in Psychology and Counseling from Sojourner Douglass College. And he has since become a student of Cognitive & Behavioral Psychology. In 2018, Darrell hosted the Conflict Resolution Show on Be Exposed Radio. In 2019 he transitioned his show into a podcast platform on the Next Chapter Radio Network and began the Relationship Conflict Group via Facebook. In 2020 he transitioned into his independent podcast called Relationship Conflict Talk, and signed a contract with the Exposure TV Network with an opportunity to broadcast internationally.

He is an Author, Speaker, Fitness Consultant, & Relationship Conflict Specialist. And in the past, Darrell has partnered with restaurants nationwide to host conversation parties where single and married couples discuss relationship conflict topics. He also partners with community organizations to provide relationship conflict groups for those that have challenges with addictions.

Darrell's education and his experiences have compelled him to embrace a more holistic approach to training which encompasses a physical, mental, and/or spiritual impact for his clients.

Nakesha White is a wife, mother, and grandmother who enjoys weaving words of resilience and healing as a poet and licensed therapist. She is known for conquering odds with ink-stained hands and a heart full of grace.

#WriterLife #PoetTherapist
#ResilienceMatters